"ESCAPE AL

I looked up and saw our faces on the viewsc~~
and suddenly I felt as if someone had kicked me
in the guts. Through a ringing in my ears, I heard:

"A male and female reported missing. Believed
together somewhere in Sectors Seven, Eight, and
Nine. Extreme caution advised. Male fugitive is
former gladiator—skills may still exist on reflex
level. Female is code nine, political, sensitive.
Under no circumstances approach fugitives.
Contact nearest State Security HQ."

I glanced at the girl. "That's it, then," I said.
"You wanted out? Okay, here's your big chance.
We move up our schedule. We make our escape
now—or never. . . ."

THE
IDENTITY
PLUNDERERS

SIGNET Science Fiction You'll Enjoy

— THE —
IDENTITY
PLUNDERERS

Isidore Haiblum

A SIGNET BOOK
NEW AMERICAN LIBRARY

Copyright©1984 by Isidore Haiblum

 SIGNET TRADEMARK REG. U.S. PAT. OFF. AND FOREIGN COUNTRIES
REGISTERED TRADEMARK—MARCA REGISTRADA
HECHO EN CHICAGO, U.S.A.

SIGNET, SIGNET CLASSIC, MENTOR, PLUME, MERIDIAN and
NAL BOOKS are published by New American Library
1633 Broadway, New York, New York 10019

First Printing, March, 1984

1 2 3 4 5 6 7 8 9

PRINTED IN THE UNITED STATES OF AMERICA

— CHAPTER —
One

The buzzing sliced through my mind.

My eyelids jerked open.

I was lying on a hard metal bunk, staring up at a metal ceiling. I'd been dreaming something. But I didn't know what.

"Rise," a metallic voice intoned through the communo-grille.

I got to my feet. I didn't want to argue with that voice. The spotter-eye, high up near the ceiling, saw all, knew all. To disobey would mean instant punishment: metal was a dandy conductor of electricity.

I kept my arms by my sides, my gaze fixed on the wall. I tried to make my face a blank, empty thing. *Like the others.*

The bars silently slid back into the wall.

I did a left face, shuffled out into the corridor. I had lots of company. On either side of me, as far as my eye could see, Blanks in coarse gray workclothes stood listlessly at attention. Most looked like men. The Northern Galaxies had been settled eons ago by menlike entities. A fact that shouldn't have been kicking around my cranium but was. When it came to nonmen—one in a thousand—I tried to give them lots of room. They were creepy.

"Move," the voice commanded.

We turned right as one. We moved.

The long procession veered left, started down one of the thirty ramps. Above and below me, I knew, on fifty other levels, rows of Blanks—stoop shouldered, feet dragging, eyes staring forward—shuffled along as I did. It was a pleasant thought.

At the cleansing circle three hundred of us used the toilets, depilatories, and automat wash, changed into fresh clothes in the drying chamber, and shuffled out toward the mess hall. The next shift was already at our heels.

We stood at long tables. The feeding belt served up a gray tasteless nutritive gruel. We had three minutes to gulp it down. No utensils. We lifted the metal bowls to our lips, poured the stuff down our throats. The bell chimed. We left the tables, shuffled back to the ramps, continued our trek toward outdoors and the work zone.

We trudged through the flat, barren fields, kicking up the gray dust as we moved. Brownish-gray earth lay underfoot. Overhead, a bluish sky and small twin suns looked down.

In the distance I could hear the rumble of machinery, see the tops of the giant mechs.

From wakeup to the work zone took exactly one hour and forty-five minutes. A conveyor belt would have cut the time in half. The overseers didn't seem to care. Why should they? The mechs lumbered around the clock, were never idle. It was always day on the planet of night, at least in the work zones. Ultra-beam glowers saw to that.

I climbed onto my mech—only seconds ago vacated by my swing-shift counterpart; the seat was still warm—adjusted the harness, placed the skullcap on my head. The mech—one of the smaller items in the area, only five levels tall—was a digger. I reached out with my mind, activated the controls. The digger sprang to life with a roar. It dug.

Far off, near the horizon, a city was rising. But that was another zone, another Blank unit. All I usually got to see was the holes I scooped. By the time building mechs showed up, I and my digger would be long gone.

Possibly that was part of the punishment. Only I didn't believe it. None of the other Blanks seemed to give a damn where they were, or what they did.

And I wasn't even sure why I was being punished.

But maybe I could find out.

I glanced around cautiously. Nothing to worry about. Only towering mechs in view, each with its own Blank. No guards to be seen. I wasn't surprised. Whatever had been done to the Blanks had made them harmless and docile. They sat at their posts for a full cycle without a grunt or

6

murmur. But then they never spoke in the prison either.

I got out the knife and wire spool I'd swiped from the storage bin. Using the knife, I peeled away a strip of insulation from my skullcap cord, wound one end of the wire around it.

I took a deep breath. My hands were clammy and I could feel the sweat soaking through my clothes.

I fumbled with the harness, slipped out of the seat. As my feet hit the ground, the digger sighed to a halt.

I leaned weakly against the silent mech. Take it easy, I told myself. This isn't the first time you've gone off on a stroll. But it *was* the first time I'd bolted my mech. And it was giving me the willies.

The digger, I saw, was still surrounded by other mechs, all pumping away. Nothing to stir up the guards—yet. But in five minutes the pipelayer would wheel off toward another site. My digger would be exposed then. And if it wasn't digging, I was sunk.

I got moving, unwound the spool as I went, trailing wire behind me. I wasn't feeling so hot, but I was going to feel a lot worse if I didn't hustle. I dodged the hitter, a squat mech pounding a metal beam into the ground, skirted the piper, and keeping the adhesive mixer between me and the guard post, reached another digger.

So far, so good.

I looked up at the Blank. He seemed no different from the others. I didn't bother saying hello.

Using the stirrup, I hoisted myself to his level. The Blank ignored me. Every few minutes he might check a dial, adjust a lever, but aside from that, nothing.

I took his skullcap cord, sliced away part of the insulation, attached my wire to it. The Blank's head slowly swiveled toward me. We stared at each other. He turned back to his dials and levers; he'd lost interest.

Across the site my digger began to rumble, come to life.

I hopped down. My mech was working all right, but not digging up a storm; it was running at half speed. So was this one. Only who would notice? I couldn't remember an inspector visiting a site under construction. But my memory was nothing to brag about. It didn't matter, I had no choice. A dead mech would be a sure giveaway.

The wire connecting both diggers lay on the ground. A

moving mech could easily snap it in two. But I'd run out of brainstorms. Maybe luck would lend a hand; I had it coming.

I turned, began weaving my way through the machinery. I kept one eye peeled for guards, the other for roving mechs. It wouldn't do to get squashed like a bug or hammered into the ground now that I was so close to making my move.

The last guard post came and went. No trouble slipping past. Blanks weren't known for taking off on their own. Every once in a while, a Blank might go berserk or simply burn out. Then the guards would turn up, cart him away. And he would either be "fixed" or vanish forever.

The ground sloped down. I began to run—feebly. It had been a long time. My wind was gone and my knees felt unhinged. For a Blank I was probably setting a record. For anyone else, I was close to a washout.

I glanced back. The site was behind me, only mech tops visible. I was running in a blue-gray desert. A few stones and pinkish vegetation underfoot—otherwise nothing. I was the only moving object around, a nice target for any stray guards.

Far ahead was another site I'd helped build. Only half done. Some foulup in the pipeline had led to a standstill. The system here wasn't perfect. I was counting on that.

My legs and lungs gave out at the same time. I sank to the ground. I didn't try getting up. I did the smart thing, lay there and waited for my strength to return.

I still had the desert to myself. Gray clouds had begun to form overhead, blotting out one of the twin suns. A wind was rising.

I sighed. The wire stunt I'd pulled back at the work zone wasn't half bad. Only one small point bothered me. I couldn't figure out how I'd known the gimmick would work. Or what in the world had made me think of it.

After a while, I got up, continued hiking. No doubt about it, this Blank business wasn't geared to keeping a man in tip-top shape. I began to wonder just how long Blanks lasted on the job. I had a feeling I wouldn't like the answer.

I hit the old construction site about half an hour later. I stood there looking around, trying to get my bearings.

The pipes, foundation, dugouts were rusted. Blue-gray sand had washed over the works. I couldn't remember how long ago I'd been here. But there were so many things I didn't know that one more hardly mattered. I shrugged it off and got busy.

The storage shed was half buried under a mound of sand. I had to sweat some to get the door open. Dark inside. I smelled oil, moldy canvas, damp wood, plasto-deck and a number of odors I couldn't place.

Slowly I made my way across the rotting floorboards. And with each step my scheme began to seem more woozy. If I thought about it long enough, I'd probably junk the whole plan. I stopped thinking about it.

The large wooden crates were where I'd last seen them, over in the right-hand corner. As far as I could tell, they hadn't been touched. All of them contained spare parts for the mechs. All except one.

I got hold of the top crate and shoved. I was surprised by how heavy it was. I'd lost a lot of ground riding that damn mech.

I leaned into the crate, felt it begin to slide. It crashed to the floor. I didn't bother inspecting the damage; it was no concern of mine. I got busy on the next crate. Five crates down and I reached my prize.

I lifted the lid, peered inside. By now my eyes had grown used to the dark. But I still had trouble spotting the items I wanted. Most of the box contained the usual hardware. I rummaged under one metal part, then another. My fingers touched soft cloth. My lips broke into a grin, the first I could remember.

Possibly I had a chance after all.

— CHAPTER —
Two

Ross Block looked down at the body.

The face had been bashed in as though someone had taken a baseball bat to it. The features were a pulpy mess, totally indistinguishable.

The hands were gone too, chopped off at the bony wrists.

The sparse blond hair, though, was still neatly parted on the right. The guy, Block saw, had used some kind of stickum on it that had withstood not only the beating, but — according to the coroner — three days in the drink. Some stickum.

Two small, round holes punctuated the guy's narrow chest. The cause of death.

Block felt his stomach start to churn and looked away. He wasn't the only one.

"Had enough?" Rollings asked.

The assistant coroner didn't wait for an answer, pulled the sheet back over the cadaver.

Block and his sixteen press colleagues followed Rollings out of the "icehouse." The chill air and the smell of death seemed to reach after them regretfully, as though saddened by the prospect of losing so many bodies.

Block didn't pay much attention to Rollings' spiel back up in his office. The cops had gone over the same ground less than a half hour ago.

"John Doe" had been fished out of the Hudson late yesterday morning. He had on a red-and-white-checkered flannel shirt, faded jeans and worn sneakers. His pockets were empty. Someone had gone to a lot of trouble to make him unidentifiable. Three days afloat in the river had completed the job. The cops figured it for a gangland slaying.

It was the kind of story that would grab the headlines for a day or two, and then, in the absence of progress, vanish altogether. It was the kind of story Block didn't like.

"Death was caused instantly," Dr. Rollings was saying, "by the entrance of a thirty-two-caliber slug directly under the heart."

The slide projector snapped on and the reporters were looking at a blown-up picture of the cadaver's chest. Mercifully, Block saw, the image stopped short of the head.

Rollings used a pointer, jabbed at the two bullet holes as he talked. Block didn't take notes. The rupturing of the aorta or this and that vein held little interest for the *Register*'s readers. The finding of the body, its mutilated condition, and what the police had to say about it all would turn them on. Block figured he could write the piece in his sleep; he'd done it often enough.

Most of his colleagues seemed to share his boredom; some were doodling, others whispering to each other, the majority seemed lost in thought.

Block glanced back at the screen.

A new slide had been placed in the machine, one enlarging the bullet holes.

Block's gaze started to drift across the room, all on its own, when something caught his attention.

At first he thought it was only a smudge on the projector lens, or an imperfection on the slide itself.

But it wasn't.

The mark he was staring at, directly below the collarbone, appeared to be a very tiny six-edged star.

Ross Block felt his hands start to turn very cold.

Rollings was a medium-sized man in his mid-sixties. His once brown hair was turning gray, his thick mustache was almost white. Small hazel eyes hid behind thick glasses. His back was slightly stooped, and he walked with an ambling gait.

Block followed him down the corridor. They waited patiently for the elevator to show up.

"How old was the guy?" Block asked.

"Tsk, tsk," Rollings said. "You weren't paying attention, Mr. Block. Our guest was all of thirty-five, give or take a few years. It's hard to say precisely, you see, under these conditions."

The elevator doors rumbled open; they stepped in, were carried down to the basement.

Block followed Rollings along a narrow aisle. The morgue's "ice room" was just that—icy. Block stuffed his hands into his pants pockets. The odor of death and decay crept out to welcome them as if they were dear, cherished friends. Block could taste something bitter in his mouth. Whatever notion had prompted him to come back was fading fast.

They rounded a bend. The stiffs here were laid out on pale-green stretchers, six to a tier.

"Last stop, Mr. Block."

Rollings jerked the sheet off the John Doe cadaver.

Block moved closer, stared down at the body, tried to ignore the two jagged stumps, the pulverized face that looked like raw chopped meat. He concentrated on the tiny, almost invisible scar. . . .

He could see the Brooklyn schoolyard in his mind's eye, the handball court off to the right, the five-story red brick school behind it—looking like some large penitentiary—and beyond that the peeling tenements, screeching el above dark, shadowed streets, small cluttered stores and occasional supermarkets.

All this was years ago. He couldn't have been older than eleven or twelve. From time to time a bunch of the guys used to meet in the yard for stickball or some other game. Marty Nash was Nick Siscoe's pal, and he didn't show up very often. In two years, Nash and Block had hardly exchanged more than a dozen words.

That particular day, the guys chose up sides for touch football. Nash was on the other team. The game got rough. Somewhere along the way Nash tripped Block. He went down hard on the concrete, ripped his pants, skinned a knee and came up fighting mad.

A lot of the early days blend into each other, are lost to conscious memory. Except for a few standouts. Block's tussle with Nash was one of these.

Nash was faster than Block, knew a thing or two about boxing. For a while he held his own. But all his dodging and fancy footwork eventually wore him out.

Block landed a right high on Nash's chest, a left to his stomach. A right to the head spun Nash sideways. And a hard right put him down.

That was it. The guys stepped in, broke it up.

The ring Block wore that day had done more damage than any blow he struck. It left two tiny scars on Nash: one on his chin, the other under his left clavicle. *Both in the shape of a six-edged star.*

Rollings grinned at Block. "Spellbinding, isn't it?"

Block snapped out of his reverie. "Yes," he said. "About as cheerful as getting your head caught in a meat grinder."

"So what did you find out, Mr. Block?"

"That I should've let well enough alone."

The sheet went back over John Doe's last remains; Rollings and Block headed for the exit.

"I must say, Mr. Block, that your devotion to duty is an inspiration."

"Knock it off, Rollings. I was just getting a fix on the gruesome details."

Rollings winked. "Perhaps you'd like to sit in on the autopsy?"

"Let's not get carried away."

The elevator took them up.

"How do you stand it, Rollings?"

"It's steady work, Mr. Block; you can't beat that."

"When's the autopsy?"

"Tomorrow morning."

"I'll call you."

"I thought you might."

— CHAPTER —

Three

Sector Eight was jumping, all right.

I stood behind the force fence which led into the main zone and took in the sights. No machines waddled along here, no Blanks marched listlessly in file. The plasto-deck buildings were clean, modern, dome-shaped, freeform or

13

rectangular; few were more than twenty levels tall. Small two-seaters scooted along the express ramps. Pedestrians of both sexes hiked on the walkways. Even the sky seemed cheerful overhead. No one at first glance would take this place for a prison. But that's what it was.

The medallion I had in my pocket would unlock the fence, let me through. And my dark-blue uniform with the two gold stripes on the left sleeve would ensure that no one got in my way. All I had to do was take the first step. All wasn't that easy.

I stood rooted to the spot. My head seemed out of sync with my body. The whole thing was going to be too much for me. I was starting to miss my digger. Any second now, the maties behind the fence would get a treat, see an Overseer fall flat on his face.

I rummaged through my mind trying to find a key that might dampen the turmoil. There was none.

I took a deep breath, reached for the medallion, pressed it against the code slot. The fence parted and I stepped through.

In a matter of minutes I was lost in the crowd, strolling along an upper walkway. My breathing slowly went back to normal, my knees stopped shaking. No one paid any attention to me. Sector Eight held over a hundred thousand maties. I was just another Overseer on the prowl. An at-large shield on my belt clip and a Warder's pass in my hip pocket gave me the run of the place.

I was all set.

Almost.

The D building—for Directorate—was the tallest structure in the zone. Twenty-four solid, windowless levels rose off the ground. A pair of gray-clad sentries stood at each of the four arched doorways. It was a dandy spot to keep away from.

Stepping up to the main entrance, I flashed my shield. The stolid, expressionless guard didn't seem too impressed. He didn't club me with his laser, either. I went in.

A wide, mobile staircase took me to the first level. From there I boarded a speed-lift, was whisked to level eighteen. My shield got me past another checkpoint. The last leg of my jaunt had me waving my Warder's pass. It did the trick.

"This way, sir."

I followed him down a short corridor. He was small, fat, with radish ears and watery eyes. He ran a sub-bureau which took up two levels, and had at least a couple of hundred flunkies. And he called me "sir." I wondered what crime the little man had pulled to land here. And if somehow I'd manage to beat him to the outside.

We halted in front of a force door. The small man's medallion got us through a large domed hall. The left wall was all computer. Techs were busy at it. Smaller terminals were placed throughout the hall. Techs sat at desks, long and short workbenches, twirling dials, punching keys, jerking levers. The activity hardly looked more uplifting than my stint on the mech.

"If you'll wait here, sir, I'll go and fetch her."

I watched him hurry down the aisle, stop at a desk, bend over to speak to a girl with long blond hair. She looked up, saw me. Her eyes widened. What little color she had drained from her face. She rose awkwardly; her hand automatically reached for a switch. Her terminal went dark. She followed the small man back toward me.

"Here she is, sir. I place her in your charge."

I nodded. "Don't worry. I'll have her back by curfew."

"Sir, it was never my intention to imply—"

I raised a hand, silenced him.

I took the girl by the elbow, steered her down the corridor.

So far it was simple.

We left the building, headed into the crowd. We hadn't swapped a syllable yet. The Directorate was loaded with magneto-ears, spotter-eyes. A wrong word would have had us both in a cell in a matter of seconds.

I led the blonde deeper into the crush of hurrying maties. We moved along the midwalk. A couple of guards passed us. Neither showed any interest in me or the girl. I didn't kid myself. It was too soon for congratulations. I'd merely traded one prison for another, not made it over the wall.

The girl said, "I did not think you would ever come." Her voice was low, husky. She had green eyes, a long regal neck. Her features were even, skin surprisingly smooth. Being on the Penal World hadn't aged her—yet.

"You weren't the only one," I told her.

"What happened?"

"I was sick."

"They knew?"

"I wouldn't be here if they had. As long as I could drag myself to the damn digger, I was safe. Probably looked more like a Blank than ever. Trouble was, it almost killed me."

The girl was shocked. "You were wearing out. *And managed to control it?*"

"Yeah, wearing out. Look," I grinned, "we've been through this before. I'm not *that* bad off, or I wouldn't be here; okay?"

The girl nodded. But she didn't have her heart in it. For her I was still some kind of high-class Blank. Possibly she was right.

"Do you remember your crime yet?" she asked breathlessly.

I shook my head. "I'm lucky to remember your face."

"But more *has* come to you?"

"Some. While I was sick."

"It will help us?"

I shrugged. "Can't tell yet. It's tough sorting it out. I'm not sure what's important, what isn't."

"Then *why* are you here?"

"Why not? At least I can walk again. We have to start sometime. It might as well be now."

There were no sentries at the nondescript structure we came to some twenty-five minutes later. It was a five-level plasto-deck rectangle. The plaque over the door read: Data Control. The door wasn't locked. I turned to the girl. "Just follow me. Mum's the word. This whole place is full of magneto-ears."

The girl nodded. We went in.

The middle-aged lady at the desk—a matie herself—glanced up from her terminal, took in my uniform and went back to her work. Nothing like a uniform to inspire respect—especially in a prison.

The girl and I passed a long row of viewscreens, a pair of browsers, a scruffy terminal bank. The speed-lift took us to the basement. Empty floors, two washrooms and a number of closed doors. I didn't see any spotter-eyes.

The girl and I exchanged glances. If she was wondering

16

what next, she wasn't the only one. I was pretty sure I had the right building. Again and again I'd sorted through the facts in my mind. They all pointed toward this location. My mental diagram stopped short in the basement.

I closed my eyes, leaned up against the wall and tried very hard to *think*.

I had never been able to force the mind-flow, make the clicks come on demand. Now was no exception. I sighed, and did the next best thing, began trying doors. The ones that opened led either to a closet or an empty room. The locked ones stayed locked. I wasn't too worried about that, I was merely taking stock. In all, twelve doors were sealed shut. I got down on my hands and knees and started looking. The lack of spotter-eyes was encouraging. If this was the place, the big boys wouldn't want anyone spying on them.

I was midway through my search when I heard the footsteps. The girl stiffened. I didn't bother getting to my feet. I was an Overseer.

A burly man carrying a tray of computer disks poked his head around a corner, did a double take, said, "Sir. May I be of service?"

"It's okay," I said, waving him on. He didn't have to be told twice. I heard the disks sliding into a bin, the matie's footsteps fading. I grinned at the girl. She didn't grin back. She was busy biting her lip. She had a point, at that. I got busy again. After a while I found the button.

We went down a very long winding staircase, smooth stone walls on either side of us. Small white ceiling lights snapped on as we passed underneath, then went dark again. The setting seemed both strange and familiar, a feeling I was rapidly getting used to. And not liking one bit.

The girl touched my shoulder. I turned my head. Her green eyes were wide, questioning. I knew what she wanted.

"Go on," I told her. "It's okay to talk now."

Her voice was a whisper. *"Why?"*

"Why not? It's safe."

"I do *not* understand." She sounded peevish. I could sympathize. Up above no place was ever safe from the watchers and listeners.

"This is restricted territory," I explained. "Been here for ages. Only the top brass ever shows up."

The girl just stared at me.

"Sorry," I said, "we'll take it from scratch. Where we are now is run by the Galactic Arm. Each of the planets the Arm controls has a setup like this. It's strictly off limits to most of the natives; only a handful would even know about it—along with a couple of Arm liaison officers. Get it?"

The girl hesitated. "What is the Arm?"

"Oh, brother," I said, "you've got to be kidding—" And stopped. We'd rounded a bend, hit bottom.

White lights blazed at us, made me shield my eyes.

The girl gasped.

I didn't blame her. It was something to see, all right.

I took her hand, stepped over the threshold.

The room was circular. The long white table with twelve padded chairs stood at its center. The wall—with the sole exception of the doorway—was one immense computer: dials, levers, knobs, viewscreens, keyboard, the works.

"Where *are* we?"

"The Data Bank—where else? Bet it feels just like home. Everything you've always wanted to know about this world, and then some. We have a direct channel to the Control World, too. That one we ignore. We can monitor surface transmissions, get a line on any matie, even take a crash course in Galactic history."

The girl bit her lip. "Forgive me. Galactic Arm. Control World. These words are . . . *strange* to me."

I looked at her.

"I know only my duties, my dorm sisters, the allowed areas. I do not even know my crime. I can only vaguely recall being anywhere else. But, of course, that is part of the punishment, is it not?"

I shook my head uneasily. I thought I'd had this zone down pat, knew its ins and outs. Guess again. I wondered what else I'd gotten wrong.

I said, "You've *got* to know more than that."

"But I do not!"

"Come on, you trying to tell me that all your co-workers have had their minds erased?"

"They are different from me."

"How?"

"They *remember* more. They still have hope. They can recall their homes, their friends even. Although they are not

18

permitted to speak of this. Their crimes were surely less than mine."

"But you don't recall your crime?"

"No."

"You remembered *me* when we first met, didn't you?"

"Yes . . . no . . . I am not certain. It was as if a fog had parted. But that could not be—"

"It couldn't. Only I felt it too."

"How is that possible?"

"That's the whopper, all right, the one that pulls down the big prize."

It had been my first and only other jaunt to Sector Eight. Supplies had run short at the work zone. The Blanks were kept busy hauling crates. No one noticed when I slipped away.

I was in full uniform, one I'd borrowed, along with a shield, medallion and Warder's pass, from the nearest security bin. The clicks had been coming thick and fast, working overtime, and the bin code had clicked into my mind right on cue.

I'd cased Sector Eight's main zone, made sure I had its layout memorized and was getting set to start back when I saw her. She was on a midwalk, part of the crowd, headed my way.

Something clicked in my mind; it was a lulu of a click, almost knocking me silly.

I got my legs working, managed to move in front of her. She looked up. Our eyes met. And locked. I was sweating plenty.

"Come with me," I heard myself say.

She came.

The rec park had grass, trees, benches, strolling maties. What it didn't have were magneto-ears, spotter-eyes. Some Overseer had been feeling generous.

We went down an empty walkway.

I said, "You recognized me, didn't you? And it wasn't from here."

Her mouth opened, closed. No words came out. She stared at me with her large green eyes. "Sir," she finally said, "I . . . I . . . do not know. . . ." She looked as though she was going to pass out.

"Who are you?" I said.

That got me nothing.

I said, "What do you do?"

She told me, haltingly.

And as she spoke the mind-flow swept over me like a wave. I could hear her every word, but something was clicking away in my head. It wouldn't stop. An idea began taking shape along with the clicks.

Silence told me she was done.

It was my turn. I started speaking quietly. "Don't let this uniform fool you. I'm a matie, like you. Worse yet—a Blank."

I didn't wait for her reaction. I kept talking. I told her a couple of things about myself. And a little about my plan. There wasn't much time left. I made it short and sweet. All the while wondering how I could be doing this.

"That's it," I said when I was through.

"It."

"Yeah. You've got a choice now. You can blow the whistle on me, pray the Overseers are grateful and don't erase you for this chat. You can take your chances with me. Or forget all about our little talk. What's it going to be?"

The girl ran a shaky hand through her blond hair, blinked at me.

"Make it snappy," I said. "I need an answer from you."

"I do not understand," she complained. "Why have you chosen me . . . put your life in the hands of a . . . stranger?"

I hunted through my brain for a reason, something that might satisfy this girl. And me. "I don't know," I told her.

She didn't meet my eyes.

"I'm still waiting."

The girl hesitated. Time seemed to be frozen. A lot of it or very little went by. The walkway wound between trees. We were alone here, out of sight. I wondered whether I'd have enough guts to kill her if she came up with the wrong answer.

The girl nodded once. "Yes," she whispered so low I could barely hear her.

I let out my breath. "Where can I find you?"

"The D building. Level eighteen."

"Your name?"

"I am dorm twelve, bunk seven. I have no name."

"Is that standard?"

She shrugged.

"What do I call you?"

"Do not call me anything."

"Why?"

"I will not be called by a number."

"You could make up a name."

"No!"

"Okay, I'll be in touch."

The girl said, "Our minds . . . are so . . . incomplete."

"Possibly." I jerked a thumb at the wall-sized computer. "But what we can't remember, this baby can."

"We will surely be discovered."

"No chance. The Bank's top priority, used only in a pinch. We could camp here for months and no one'd be the wiser."

"You are certain?"

"I'd bet my life on it."

"And I am here simply because you feel we have met before?"

"Generous of me, isn't it?"

"There is more, though."

"Sure. Just because I know about this place, the Galactic Arm, doesn't mean I'm a walking encyclopedia. Lots of things I don't know." I waved an arm toward the computer. "And how to run that damn mech is one of them."

Four

They were paging Block on the loudspeaker.

He closed the Manhattan phonebook—no Marty Nash was in it—then got to his feet and headed for the city desk.

Around him the city room hustled and bustled. Block's colleagues typed away at their word processors, batting out their latest stories. Editors shuffled through reams of copy. Phones rang. Reporters wandered up and down the aisles. The air was thick with cigarette, cigar and pipe smoke. A thin slice of cloudy sky peered in through grimy windows. The day wasn't half done, but already the floor was littered with cigarette butts, crumpled pieces of paper, sandwich wrappers. The *Register* wasn't exactly noted for running a tight ship.

"What's up, Ben?" Block asked.

Ben Cohen, the city editor, took his half-chewed cigar out of his mouth, grinned up at Block and said, "Nice job on that cadaver."

"Piece of pie." Block pulled up a hard-backed chair, sat down.

"Got something else for you. Real easy."

"That'll be the day."

Cohen leaned back in his swivel chair. He was a short, round-faced man of about sixty-two, with a potbelly, thick hairy arms and a balding dome. "Dame got herself mugged last night. East Eighty-ninth Street. About eleven-ten."

"Fascinating. What rotten thing have I done to deserve this windfall?"

Cohen raised a hand. "Hear me out, son. Lady ran home, lived half a block away, got her bike out, chased after the culprit, who was hightailing out of the neighborhood on foot, and ran him down."

"With the bike?"

"Uh-huh."

"Jesus. What happened?"

"She broke a leg."

"And the guy?"

"The miscreant fled into the night. On the lady's bike."

"Hmmmm. The tale *does* have possibilities."

Cohen grinned. "Did I ever steer you wrong, Ross?"

"Sure, lots of times."

"But aside from those?"

"Hardly ever."

"See? Lady's named Sue Taylor. Should be back from the hospital any hour. Why don't you look her up?"

"Fine. I could use some time for a John Doe follow-up, too."

Cohen raised an eyebrow. "What's to follow up? The corpse is still as anonymous as a can of tuna fish. At least according to latest reports. You know something?"

"Could be."

"So spill it."

Block fidgeted. "Actually, I'd rather not."

"Christ, a coy reporter, of all things. I don't believe it."

"Look, Ben, I've got a hunch about this guy, more than a hunch, maybe. But the whole thing's so wacky, I don't want to go on record with it."

"So now I look like a record?"

Block grinned. "Gimme a break, Ben, a couple of days on this. I'll come clean then, no matter what."

Cohen sighed. "Go on, take what you need. But this better be good."

Nora Clifford said, "You're *what?*"

They were cuddled on Nora's oversized green-and-orange-striped couch. Block took another swig from a tall glass of tomato juice; a slice of lime bobbed around in it.

"Run it down," he said.

"That's silly."

"What isn't these days?"

Nora's head had been resting on his shoulder. Now she turned to gaze at him.

She was twenty-eight, five foot three, had a wealth of

curly light-brown hair, an oval face, pert nose, thin lips and dark-brown eyes. She wore faded jeans and a white lace-trimmed blouse and was barefoot.

Block's business attire — brown jacket, beige slacks, white shirt — hung in the closet. He was dressed in jeans and a blue denim shirt and was also barefoot.

He kissed her on the nose, got up, went to the window. Four stories down was West Broadway and Spring Street. This was Soho, the Lower Manhattan art district. Cozy bars, smart restaurants, some chic boutiques and lots of galleries competing for attention. Neon lights glowed from show windows. The voices of evening strollers drifted past Block's window, faded into the night.

"Listen," he said, "I've been waiting for some kind of break for a couple of years now."

"Sweetie, you don't know when you're well off."

"Sure I do. Think I'm a dummy?"

"So what are you complaining about?"

"I'm a malcontent."

Nora came up, put her arm around him. "You're an old grump."

"Young grump. Old grump is what I'm trying to avoid. Did I tell you I was slated for a column before the *Examiner* flopped?"

"You told me."

"Uh-huh. At least a couple of dozen times, I think. Now *that* would've been something. Still might be if I play my cards right."

"By chasing shadows?"

"By going after a long shot; it's done all the time."

She gave him a squeeze. "You *are* being silly; you didn't even recognize this old playmate of yours."

"The face, no. Who could? But that scar's as good as a fingerprint. Better even."

"Well, shouldn't you tell the police?"

"And blow my story?"

"Oh, Ross, you don't even know there *is* a story."

Block grinned. "Listen, honey. First off, someone's bound to report this guy missing, sooner or later — let's hope it's later, so I can nose around. But even if it's the wrong guy, I'd still get a good piece out of it! Through the jungle of the past, hunting my long-lost buddy. Something like that."

"Baby, that's awful."

"You're missing the point. However it turns out, this could be a first-person piece. Not just the usual crap about another shooting, another two-bit court case, another hit-and-run. That stuff can go on forever. And probably will if I don't get off my ass and do something soon. The *Register*'s blood, guts, and gore. They've got thirty guys beating the bushes for that kind of shit. Think I don't miss the *Examiner*? I was sitting pretty and didn't know it. But I know better now. And I'm going to do something about it."

Nora said, "You just don't understand, do you?"

"Understand what?"

"The corpus delicti. No hands, right?"

"Uh-huh."

"No face, right?"

"Uh-huh."

"How come?"

"Makes it tough to identify, honey."

"Right. Let's say the dead man *is* Marty Nash. What happens then?"

"I make the headlines. Get to do more than one piece. Go on to bigger and better things."

"But this killing is probably gangland."

"Probably."

"And they don't want anyone to know who the victim was, right?"

"Uh-huh."

"So while you hunt around for this Nash person, what're *they* going to do?"

"Nothing, I hope."

"Gone soft?"

"Honey, by the time they get wind of what's up, it'll be too late."

"But say they *do* find out, Ross? While you're still looking?"

"Then they will confront the power of the press."

"Meaning?"

"I run for my life."

"I don't like it."

"Listen, they'll think twice before knocking off a reporter.

25

Hell. You nail one, another takes his place. Stands to reason. I'm not some lone gumshoe, I've got a whole newspaper backing me up."

"You could get killed, Ross."

"Uh-huh."

"At least tell Mr. Cohen."

"I'll tell him."

"Promise?"

"Sure."

"I'll worry."

"I'll call you every hour, how's that? If you want, I'll carry a walkie-talkie, so we can keep in touch."

She sighed. "Enough. I've done my best."

"I appreciate it."

"Let's go to bed."

"Now you're talking."

— CHAPTER —
Five

The girl turned from the control panel, nodded uncertainly. "Got it figured?" I said.

She shrugged a slim shoulder. "I shall do my utmost."

"Can't ask for more."

She seated herself. "What first?"

"Let's see where we are. Get a map on the screen."

She typed out her instructions. One word appeared on the viewscreen: "Classified."

I heard myself curse.

The girl half swiveled in my direction, and her words came tumbling out. "I knew it would be so. Many times I had little to do in the work pool. I, too, would ask my computer questions. It is not allowed but it is done. The Overseers seem not to mind. Few of my questions were ever answered. Most were classified. Escape is *not* possible. We were foolish to even try—"

"Can it," I said. "All that's for topside. We're doing something wrong, that's all. Look for an override button."

She turned back. "I see nothing."

"Try the red knob over there."

The girl twisted the knob. Nothing happened.

"Erase the screen," I said. "Start from scratch."

This time when the girl typed her question a map sprang on the viewer. "See?"

"How did you know?"

"Let's not start that again. You're lucky to be with an expert. I'm a regular mental whiz. Someday I might even remember my name."

She didn't smile. Why should she? The spiffy uniform and day off from my digger had gone to my head, were giving me delusions of grandeur. By nightfall I'd be back in my cell rubbing shoulders with my fellow Blanks. There was no reason to start feeling cocky.

The girl sat quietly as I took in the map. The symbols didn't give me any trouble. I knew which represented checkpoints, spotter-eyes, security zones. Two ways, I saw, of making a getaway. The aboveground route was okay, if you stayed lost in the crowd, a big if. Belowground was another story. The tunnels were filled with barriers, spotter-eyes. But if those could be avoided, there were some nice possibilities.

"Try and get a printout of that map," I said. "I'll lug it back with me, see what I can learn."

"You are certain?"

"Why not?"

"If you are caught—"

"Then I'm a goner, anyway. Don't sweat it—nobody ever frisks a Blank, it's not worth the effort."

"But if the map *should* be found?"

I grinned. "And they make me spill my guts? Just tell the Overseers that you figured me for one of them. No one's going to call you on that. Maties don't talk back to a uniform. Ever."

The girl said nothing, returned to her panel, found the printout button. Our map quietly slid out, through a slot.

The girl looked at me.

"We should ask about ourselves."

"Us?"

"Yes! Who we are. Where we come from. What is our crime."

"Why not? What's your number?"

The girl merely stared at me.

"You know your number?" I asked. "Everyone's got a number somewhere. All you've got to do is know yours."

"I am dorm twelve, bunk seven."

"Great. Dorm twelve. It's got some other designation?"

She shrugged.

"Yeah," I said, "me too. I'm just a no-nothing Blank. No number, no name, no anything. And without those little items there's no way in the world you can ask this mech who we are. Sorry. I don't make the rules."

The girl lowered her eyes. She sat very still.

"You okay?"

"Yes." She looked up. "What information do you wish next?"

"Let's take a gander at the surrounding territory," I said.

The computer spewed out a number of adjacent maps. I gave them some study. The third one I came to was the prize. It only took me a second to realize I was staring at a full-fledged spaceport. That was my ticket out of here, all right. The planet itself, I knew, was too well organized to make a good hideout. Sooner or later, no matter where I holed up or what disguise I used, the Overseers would nab me. But the spaceport presented a couple of problems, too. First, I had to get there. And that meant crossing seven sectors—a lot of ground to cover, especially if the Overseers got wise to what I was doing. And if it took more than one shift they were bound to find out. But even if I somehow reached the port safely, I'd still be up a stump. My knowledge of spaceflight was nil. There was no way of knowing if it would ever click into place, or when. I was going to need help. But my list of acquaintances on this world was restricted to me and the girl.

"Find me some space pilots," I told her.

"Any special kind?"

"Yeah. Ones who aren't too far gone to still run a spaceship."

All in all we came up with a full dozen. I looked at the list glumly. My pilots were scattered across the globe, each behind a nice set of walls. I'd hoped that a couple might be on the loose, serving their time in one of the open zones. No such luck. It made sense, too. The temptation to sneak off toward the spaceport would be just about overwhelming.

"Something wrong?" the girl asked.

"They've got our pilots under lock and key. Very inconsiderate. It's tough enough busting out of a cell. But breaking into one to find some matie you've never even laid eyes on, that may be asking too much."

The girl said, "You are neglecting an even *graver* possibility."

"I'd rather not hear—"

"How many of these are useless Blanks?"

"Well, we got their names. We can run them through the mech, find out."

The girl didn't waste time.

One of our problems—recognizing these birds—was solved soon enough. Each name had a face that went with it. The mug shots sprang up on the viewscreen.

A short bio went with each matie. Most had been sent up for smuggling. Three of the twelve were politicals. Flying a spaceship was just a sideline for them. One had been a King, the second a President, and the last a Prime Minister. Their worlds and social systems had nothing in common, were galaxies apart. But each had run afoul of the Galactic Arm.

Two were Blanks, leaving us with ten, including the big shots. Of those, six were thousands of links away. I scratched them. Two were in Sector Fourteen, the other pair in Twelve. Fourteen was closer to the spaceport. Fourteen it was. Except that one of our pilots was the Prime Minister. And a big shot might rate an extra guard or two. I decided to stick with the working stiff; it seemed simpler.

"What next?"

"Let's see if we can get some printouts of Sector Fourteen cell block by cell block if possible."

The girl began typing her queries. I glanced around the room, pulled up one of the padded chairs, plunked down, and sighed.

A yellow light began to blink on the panel.

"What the hell's that?" I asked.

"An alert on the open channels."

"Yeah?"

"Some sort of emergency."

"Tune it in."

The girl twisted a knob. A screen above our heads lit up brightly. Two faces appeared on it: mine and the girl's.

— CHAPTER —

Six

Block found a parking space.

He flicked off WQXR; Rachmaninoff's Third Piano Concerto died in the speaker. He climbed out of the car, stood there, studying the old neighborhood. Nothing recognizable. He might have been in some other state, or even another country. The Brooklyn he'd known had been swept clean. No blackened tenements crowded the pavements. No clotheslines stretched across backyards. Tall, yellow brick, boxlike buildings—lower- and middle-income projects—had taken their place. The el was gone, too. He wasn't so sure it was an improvement. Block started walking. He had parked about half a mile from the school; maybe he'd spot a few landmarks.

He ambled along underneath a cloudy late-autumn sky. One project followed another, all relatively new, but a lot already showing signs of wear. He peered at passing pedestrians. Strangers all. Almost a full generation had gone by. Not reasonable to expect many of the old sights to be around. Good thing he hadn't come as a mere tourist; he'd've been disappointed. Probably he was going to be disappointed anyway.

The five-story red brick building seemed scruffier than ever. Graffiti decorated part of the east wall. The green wire mesh which covered the large windows was peeling and rusted. The schoolyard itself sported numerous cracks, which vaguely resembled varicose veins. But no doubt about it, he'd come home. Here was P.S. 67, bowed and under the weather maybe, but still pretty much as he remembered it. The place was far from abandoned; noisy kids streamed in the front doors, heads were visible at windows. The schoolyard itself held a couple of dozen youngsters. Bracing himself for the odor which seems to reside in all public schools, Block went in.

Her nose was long, her face angular and lined, her gray hair cut short. She removed her horn-rimmed glasses, stared at him from behind an ancient desk.

"I'm afraid that is *quite* impossible," she said sternly.

"Why?" Block wanted to know.

"It is against regulations." Her voice was dry and cracked, like an old leaf.

"*What* regulations?"

"The school board's, young man."

"Look, Mrs. —"

"Miss Swanson."

"Yes, Miss Swanson, I'm with the *Daily Register.*" He got his wallet out, flashed his press card at her. "And all I want to do is run down a couple of my former classmates. I'm doing a sort of nostalgia piece about what happened to the old crowd. Nothing that could possibly hurt anyone. There's no chance of its reflecting badly on the school. And I've come all the way from Manhattan —"

"Young man, I find it hard to believe that the *Register* has benign motives in any of its articles."

"Miss Swanson, believe me —"

"But that is hardly the issue. There is simply no way I can honor your request, Mr. Block. I'm sorry. I do appreciate that you traveled a good distance. But if you had bothered to phone us first, you could have spared yourself the inconvenience. Permission can only be granted from Court Street."

"Court Street."

"Precisely. The school board's administrative office."

"Uh-huh."

"Is there something more?"

"I guess not."

"Good day, Mr. Block."

If nothing else, twelve years on the job had taught Block when to call it quits. "Okay, Miss Swanson," he said, "I'll try Court Street. Thanks." He had turned to go when inspiration struck. He turned back. "Actually there *is* something you can do."

"Yes?" Miss Swanson did not seem pleased at the opportunity.

"Long as I'm here," Block said, "might as well pay my respects to some of my old teachers. Provided they're still here, of course."

"The school has seen many changes since your day, Mr. Block."

"I'm sure."

"Whom do you have in mind?"

Block reached back in his memory. He had no trouble recalling most of his high school and college teachers; a couple had even become friends. But the public school bunch was something else. They weren't exactly top-notch members of their profession; in fact, most of them stank. He managed to dredge up and rattle off several names before Miss Swanson nodded. Just in time, too. He was starting to run dry.

"Mrs. Beggly died some five years ago. Miss Aprage and Mr. Darnatto are retired. Mrs. Friedman still teaches civics. And Mr. Falton has become chairman of the physical education department. I don't know any of the others, Mr. Block. I have only been with the school nine years."

"That's fine," he said, trying to seem delighted with his two finds. "I'd be very happy to see Mrs. Friedman and Mr. Falton."

Miss Swanson flipped through some cards. "Mrs. Friedman has classes until one. But Mr. Falton is in his office right now." She gave Block the room number. He thanked her and went away.

Thomas Falton was no longer the young muscular giant Block remembered. He had put on weight, maybe 130 pounds. He now had a round double chin, a jutting belly and sparse graying hair combed over his bald dome.

"Can't say I remember you at all, kid," Falton said in a high-pitched hoarse voice.

"Class of '54," Block said.

Falton rummaged in his desk drawer, came up with a set of old dusty black attendance books. "Don't take it personal, kid," he said. "Memory was never too hot, anyway. Don't remember half the guys I had in gym. A kid grows up, he changes, right?"

Block agreed.

"So all I gotta go on is names. That ain't my strong suit."

"I know what you mean," Block said.

Falton looked up at him, grinned. "Here you are, kid, Ross Block. Gave you two *B*s and an *A*."

"Sounds about right."

Falton snapped the book closed. "Well, it's nice you could drop in, Ross. Always glad to see my ex-students. Come again next time you're in the neighborhood."

He held out a meaty hand.

"Mr. Falton," Block said, "actually, for me this is kind of a business trip."

Falton retrieved his hand. "What's that? You selling something?"

Block gave him his best smile, showed his press card. "I'm a reporter, Mr. Falton, for the *Register*."

"Is that a fact?"

"I'd like to do a piece on P.S. 67."

Falton's face turned earnest. "Graft, corruption, ah? Can't help you there, Ross. I try to mind my own business."

"Nothing like that," Block assured him. "This story would be about my class, what happened to the guys since then. And about you, too, what a fine gym class you ran, how you've gone on to become chairman."

"Well now, that sounds real nice. Read the *Register* myself. Have for years. Wouldn't miss seeing that little item."

"It was all set, until I spoke to your Miss Swanson."

"Whaddya mean?"

"My time's limited on this sort of piece. It's not especially world-shaking news. Your Miss Swanson would give me none of the addresses I need, sent me off to Court Street."

"Damn red tape," Falton said. "But those addresses are gonna be way outta date anyway."

"They're only a starting point. From here I find out what high school my guys attended. From there, jobs, maybe, or colleges. You work your way up, Mr. Falton. But this *is* base one."

"Damn red tape," Falton growled. He rose ponderously. "Have a seat, Ross. What were the names you want? I'll get 'em myself. Can't let stupid regulations botch up a story, ah? You stay put, Ross, I'll be right back."

There were five names on Block's list.

> Marty Nash
> Nick Siscoe
> Bernie Rothman
> Sally Niel
> Howard Bell

Siscoe was Nash's pal, had brought him into Block's circle.

Rothman and Bell were schoolyard regulars; they knew everyone.

Sally Niel had hung out with Siscoe.

Three of his group, it turned out, had gone to Washington High, which was only six blocks away. Block left his car where it was and walked over.

Dr. Wendell Green was a thin bird with a narrow, lined face, bushy mustache, and stooped shoulders. He was Miss Swanson's counterpart at the high school, but comparisons ended there.

"A story in the *Register?* Why not, indeed? Three students, you say? Well, that shouldn't be too hard. Merely a matter of checking our graduation records. If you can spare a few moments, I'll just go down the hall and see what can be found in our alumni files. Always a pleasure to help the press, Mr. Block. Don't get to do it very often."

Green left Block alone in his office, perched on an uncomfortable wooden chair. A small, half-empty bookshelf held an ancient Webster's, a college guide, two well-thumbed career guides, an atlas and the Brooklyn phone directory. All the furniture was institutional brown, on the battered side, and covered by a thin layer of dust. Gray light filtered through the bare window. The odor of Lysol drifted in from the hallway. Voices came from there, too, sounding young and very sappy. Block sighed. What the hell was he doing here? Something about being back in the public school—even on a visit—depressed him. The sights, sounds and smells seemed to crowd in on him. He was a kid again.

34

What was he going to be? A playwright like O'Neill? Another Hemingway? Maybe a hotshot news ace like Ed Murrow? Pulling down a Pulitzer would be a snap. And why not a Nobel Prize, too, while he was at it. Anything was possible as long as you had enough guts, talent, gumption. *No shit.*

Wendell Green came back, more stooped than ever. He sank into his chair behind the beat-up desk and wagged his head at Block. "A sad thing, Mr. Block, a very sad thing."

"Yes? What is?"

"To lose them so young."

"We've lost someone?"

"Oh yes. I'm afraid so. On the very threshold of life, as it were. A *terrible* waste."

"Which one?"

"Nicholas Siscoe."

"Siscoe, eh? Too bad." He tried to remember what Siscoe had looked like. He got a hazy picture of a big black-haired kid with a straight nose and big ears. Siscoe had been Nash's buddy, not his. If he were actually doing a piece on his school chums, these five wouldn't even rate a mention. "What happened?" Block asked.

"A traffic accident. Some ten years ago. Nicholas Siscoe was run down while crossing the street. A hit-and-run."

"Mr. Green, how do you know all this? You keep records of student deaths?"

"Dear me, no. But Mr. Siscoe was most active in the alumni association, it seems. I didn't know him personally, of course. I was teaching in the Bronx then. But Mr. Siscoe's file is quite full. He donated money annually to the alumni fund. And one year he was chairman of the fundraising committee. Someone clipped the *Post* story of his death and put it in his file."

"Could I have a copy of that?"

"Certainly."

"What have you got on the others, Mr. Green?"

"We have an address for Martin Nash in our records. But it is twenty-two years old."

"Didn't join the alumni?"

"Didn't even graduate. Dropped out in the bottom of his junior year."

"What about Sally?"

"You may have better luck with her, Mr. Block."

"A joiner?"

"Not quite. But we do try to keep track of our graduates. We send out questionnaires to all the alumni in our files, every five years, asking for information about their classmates. Sally Niel has been Mrs. Charles Hastings for the last six years. We have the address."

"Married kind of late, didn't she?"

Green shrugged. "Perhaps it was her second marriage, Mr. Block, or even her third. Who can tell?"

— CHAPTER —
Seven

I looked up at the two faces on the viewscreen and felt as if someone had kicked me in the guts. My head was spinning and the floor was tilting sideways, never a good sign. Through the ringing in my ears, I heard:

"Escape alert. Escape alert.

"A male and female reported missing. Believed together somewhere in Sectors Seven, Eight and Nine. Extreme caution advised. Male fugitive is former gladiator—skills may still exist on reflex level. Female is code nine. Under no circumstances approach fugitives. Contact nearest State Security HQ.

"Escape alert, escape alert . . ."

The robot voice started the spiel over from the start. I stopped listening. And tried to start thinking. It wasn't easy. I was still in shock. Any second I was going to keel over. I glanced at the girl. Her face had turned chalky white, her chest was heaving, and her eyes looked glazed.

I made an extreme effort and used my voice:

"Pull yourself together." It came out a whisper.

The girl shuddered. She didn't bother with an answer,

but the sound of my voice had helped her. Possibly I was going to survive the next five minutes after all.

What the hell had gone wrong?

A guard could have stumbled across my jury-rigged digger. My mug shot had been flashed over the screens. And someone had remembered me taking the girl from the D building, put two and two together.

Short, sweet—and probably fatal!

Unless I came up with something smart.

I didn't feel smart. But I wasn't going to let my feelings stand in the way.

I looked up at the viewscreen.

Neither I nor the girl had aged much since the photos were taken—so both were of recent vintage. We weren't old-timers then, but new arrivals. Which wasn't exactly news in my case. Blanks didn't last long. If I was still in okay shape, I was a newcomer. And I'd been in *great* shape before. The robot voice had called me a gladiator.

How about that?

It was possible, all right. I was around six foot two. Somewhere in my mid-thirties. My nose looked as if it had been broken once or twice. My shoulders were broad. And I had a darn sight more muscle than any other Blank I'd ever bumped into.

A gladiator ought to be a tough character to nail.

Possibly, I still had a chance. A real one.

The girl spoke. Her voice was shaking. "What is code nine?"

"Search me." I waved toward the bank. "Ask it."

The girl slowly typed the question.

Two words appeared on the viewscreen: *Sensitive. Political.*

"What do you know—you're somebody," I said.

"Somebody?"

"A big shot."

"It means *nothing.*" Her voice was bitter. "Does it tell me why I am here, what I have done? *Who I am?*"

I was getting annoyed. "Don't ask for miracles. We're way ahead of the game. You're a political, I'm a gladiator. Possibly you were on the wrong end of a coup? Maybe I threw some big fight and got caught? What could be simpler?"

"Yes, it is simple now. They have found us out. You said we would be safe. Where can we go? Only to give ourselves up. And we will be punished, *terribly punished*—"

"Forget that."

"How can I?"

"We've been through this. You were only taking orders."

"They will *never* believe me. I shall be erased. *Totally.*"

"Not if you use your head."

"What do you mean?"

"You can come with me."

"Where?"

"The spaceport and out of here."

"You are insane. We are not prepared!"

I grinned. "Think it over. The Overseers figure me for a Blank. A high-class Blank, but still a dimwit who doesn't know his ass from his elbow. That's where we've got the edge. Listen. Some stuff in my mind even the Overseers don't have. They can't know we've gotten into the Data Bank, come up with the spaceport, got a printout of the territory. You wanted out? Okay, here's your big chance. We move up our schedule. That's all. We make our play now!"

The girl bit her lip. "But what hope have we?"

"Plenty. Give yourself up and you might be okay. But it'd mean spending the rest of your life in this hole. That's no picnic. You'll have to decide for yourself. Me, I don't have much choice. This time, if I get caught, they won't make any mistakes, they'll erase me for keeps. A vegetable would seem bright by comparison. I've got to move on with or without you. What's it going to be?"

The girl stared at me. Her eyes seemed bigger, greener now. I sat back, gave her time to mull it over.

The escape alert was still yakking away. I was getting tired of looking at myself. I got up and snapped it off. The silence that followed seemed to slam down on me like a lid. There was no sound at all, as if the girl and I were suspended in time. What the hell, I wondered, was I talking about? Get to the spaceport? I'd be lucky to get out of the building.

The girl broke the silence, her voice low. "I will go with you," she said.

"You sure?"

She nodded.

"Why?"

"I am afraid I will not stand up under questioning."

"Don't be silly."

"No. It does not matter. I *wish* to go with you."

"You absolutely certain?"

"Yes."

I shrugged. "Okay, you're on."

The girl's eyes met mine. "I *do* believe we might succeed. I was afraid, *am* afraid, but what you have done is . . . is . . . *incredible.*"

"Thanks. I'd feel a lot better if I could figure out *how* the hell I did it."

"It is not important."

"Could be. But we've still got a long way to go. I don't know how well I'm going to hold up. We may run out of luck."

"Now it is *you* who is pessimistic. It is not luck. It is something else, entirely."

"Like what?"

"I do not know."

"That makes two of us."

The girl smiled. The first time I'd seen her do that. She said, "I am glad we recognize one another, that you chose me."

"Thought we recognized."

"More than that. I will not blame you if we fail. This life is impossible. It is a living death. You were right: *anything* is better."

The girl worked at the keyboard. I paced up and down, pausing now and then to examine some part of our layout. It told me nothing. I hoped the computer would tell me more. I wanted detailed close-ups of the spaceport, Sector Fourteen, the belowground tunnels. The more, the better.

"How's it coming?" I asked.

"We have more data than we shall ever need."

"A bit more won't hurt. We'll be making our big play in Sector Fourteen. We'll want to know how many Warders, Overseers, and security-traps are stacked against us; check it."

The girl frowned. "It will take time."

"Time is what we've got."

"But surely it is not wise to remain here so long. Not now, when they seek us."

"It's safe enough. This is the one place they'll never look. It's when we hit topside our troubles begin."

"And you are attempting to *postpone* these troubles?"

"I wouldn't mind — if I could figure out how."

"Then why do we remain here?"

"Simple. We're waiting for it to get dark."

"Dark?"

"Yeah. My guess is the building upstairs empties out around nightfall. That's when all the maties go home. Then we take off. The darkness will help us. We've got some ground to cover topside before we reach the tunnel."

The girl was looking at me sharply. "We were seen in this building, in the basement as well. They will have to search for us here."

"Sure. But the folks doing the hunting don't even know this place exists. Remember? And their bosses don't know either. We're just a political and a gladiator, right? By the time the big shots who run this world get into the act, we'll be long gone. That's the plan, anyway."

"I am worried."

"Who isn't?"

"How can you be so certain we are insignificant?"

"Easy. They wouldn't have had me guiding a digger and you hacking away at a terminal if we were important. Makes sense?"

"Perhaps. But there is still one question unexplained."

I smiled. "You mean how does a mere gladiator come to know about this setup?"

"*Yes!*"

"Beats me."

An hour slipped by without much fuss. The girl was still coaxing answers out of the Data Bank, and I was sweating over its handiwork, trying to put together a scheme that might get us safely off planet and headed toward other worlds — any would do — when the red light over the doorway started to blink.

I stared at it stupidly.

Something began to click in my head as though old and atrophied synapses had suddenly come alive. I knew the

40

meaning of the blinking light, all right, had known it from the start.

"We've got visitors," I told the girl, trying to keep my voice calm.

She whirled around to face me, eyes wide, mouth open.

"Don't ask me why or how, but we've got 'em. They're working their way down the staircase."

"But you said—"

"Yeah. You can sue me later—if there is a later."

"We must—"

"Shhh," I told her. I glanced around the circular room, waiting for the click to come again and tell me where to find a hidden door, a passageway to lead us out of here. Nothing happened.

I could feel the sweat starting to coat my body.

I'd come a long way from my digger during the last ten hours, but obviously not far enough. I'd reached the end of the line before I'd even gotten into play. I'd learned a lot of useless junk. And found out I'd once been a gladiator. That was as close as I'd ever come to knowing who I was. By tomorrow, provided I was still among the living, I'd know as much about myself and my surroundings as a toadstool. *I wasn't going to let that happen.* My panic was gone. Anger had taken its place.

"Stay behind me," I told the girl. "But not too close."

Three strides had me through the doorway.

I started up the stairs.

The viewscreens had warned that I might be dangerous, that my old skills might still be lurking just below the surface. We'd see soon enough.

The staircase wound around and around like a corkscrew. I ran up it—soundlessly—on the balls of my feet. Surprise was my ace. Whoever they were, my visitors wouldn't be expecting an attack from this direction. *Or would they?*

I heard their voices before I saw them. If they were trying to attract attention, they were succeeding. At least two raised voices, possibly three.

I glanced back. The girl was out of sight, well behind me.

I put on some speed, felt my muscles tense. I was starting to shake. I wasn't sure I could go up against the average cripple, let alone three normal men. Suddenly it seemed crazy for an ex-Blank to take on this kind of trouble. What I ought to do was get down on my knees and beg for mercy.

I rounded a bend.

There were four, not three, and the look on their faces was one of pure amazement.

They froze in their tracks, and it didn't take a genius to see why.

The first was tall, thin, stooped-over, and seventy if he was a day. The pair behind him looked better fed and a good ten years younger, which put them in their mid-sixties. The fatso bringing up the rear was a scale tipper well over two hundred pounds. He was younger than his pals—maybe in his late forties—but it wouldn't do him much good. He looked soft as a buttered roll, and the mere act of climbing *down* the stairs had him huffing and puffing.

I saw all this in an eyeblink. That's all the time I had for stock-taking. I didn't know if these lads were armed, if any second one of them might whip out a blaster. I moved.

My right shot out, connected with tall and skinny's chin.

He fell down.

I stepped over him.

The two middle-aged lads had neglected to move a muscle so far; they were peering at me as if trying to make sure I wasn't some apparition brought on by a bad case of indigestion.

I proved I was real by banging their heads together.

One fell to his knees.

The other lifted both arms to protect his head. I gave him an open-hand slice to the neck. He keeled over sideways.

I kicked out with my foot three times. The man on the floor closed his eyes and went to sleep.

That left fatso.

Fatso had shrewdly turned tail, was clambering up the stairs. His bulk proved a hindrance. He'd covered three steps when I got to him, grasped his jacket from behind, yanked him back.

Fatso yowled.

I put an end to the noise by slamming my fist twice into the side of his jaw. He joined his three pals in slumberland.

I stood looking down at the results of my labors. Not bad. I'd hardly worked up a sweat. On the other hand, the competition had left something to be desired. I didn't think it would take a gladiator to mop up this crew. An ordinary weakling with a bit of get-up-and-go could've done just as well.

"You have *killed* them," the girl said.

I almost jumped out of my shoes at the sound of her voice. During the fracas I'd forgotten all about her. She was down about five steps, one hand resting against the wall. She looked a bit shaky.

"They'll live," I said.

The sound of my voice surprised me. It seemed hard, cold, distant. I wasn't sure I liked that voice, or the man who went with it.

"You *must* be a gladiator," the girl said.

"Never doubted it," I said. "The Data Bank wouldn't give us a bum steer; it knows its stuff."

Stooping, I began to frisk the four sleeping oldsters. My hands moved through their pockets slowly, mechanically. I found no weapons, no identification that meant anything to me. But I knew what we had here: *the top brass.* What I didn't know was what to do with them. My mind was off somewhere else, going great guns.

I saw myself clear as day in a large stadium. There were lights, cameras, a roaring crowd, and I was the star attraction. They had me in center ring and I was polishing off one opponent after another. The scene was shooting by too fast for me to note much detail. My moves seemed interesting, but I couldn't quite pin them down.

Possibly my current bout had brought the memory back. But a sour note kept nagging at me:

What if the memory was so much eyewash, no more than a cock-and-bull story, a fantasy that found its way into my brain and lodged there? What if none of this had ever happened to me, but something, or someone, wanted me to believe it had?

I shook my head, tried to clear it. None of this made any sense. Who would waste so much effort on a Blank?

And why?

Eight

He walked over the couple of blocks to Marty Nash's old address.

The eroding projects were left behind. This avenue showed progress of another kind. The mom-and-pop stores of yesterday, with their sharp odors and narrow, cluttered aisles, were gone. Cut-rate stores filled the block now. Their chintzy wares — beach towels, Brillo pads, rag dolls — spilled out onto the sidewalks. McDonald's, Chicken Delight, and Burger King hustled for the fast-food buck. Look-alike supermarkets — Shopwell, A & P, Pioneer — slashed nickels and dimes off selected items, trying to pull in an extra customer. Block hadn't been crazy about the old neighborhood, but at least people knew each other, shopkeepers took pride in their stock. All past history now. The place had as much charm as a brick wall.

Nash had lived on this very street, but change, Block saw, had miraculously sidestepped his old building.

He stood gazing with some wonder at what was left of a decaying five-story tenement. A rickety, peeling fire escape stretched the length of the building. Most of the windows were sealed shut with squares of tin. One set of windows still had curtains and a couple of flower pots resting on its sills.

Block went up four crooked wooden steps, pushed open the door. It was dark inside, stank of urine, mold and roaches. The mailboxes were broken and gutted husks. One bore a piece of soiled adhesive tape on its lid. The name Mophet was penciled on it.

Block walked up two flights of shaky stairs, down a peeling, lopsided hallway. He rapped on the wooden door.

Nothing happened, then a scratchy male voice said, "Yeah?"

"Mr. Mophet?"

"Who is it?" The voice sounded quarrelsome.

"My name's Ross Block, Mr. Mophet; I'm with the *New York Register*. May I have a word with you?"

"No."

Nothing like a man who knew his own mind, Block thought. "Mr. Mophet," he called.

"Go away!"

"I'm willing to pay for your time."

"You're what?"

"How'd you like five bucks, Mr. Mophet?"

Block heard slow footsteps from inside. The door creaked open.

He was a small, shriveled man, with sunken, white-stubble-coated cheeks, a crooked nose, toothless gums. He wore a striped-red-and-green polo shirt, gray wrinkled pants and slippers. "Let's see the color of your dough, mister."

Block slipped him the five-spot.

The oldster glared at it suspiciously as if convinced Block had printed it himself, squinted at Block and said, "So, whaddya wanna know?"

"You live here alone?"

"No, share the place with the Queen of England."

"How long you lived here?"

"Thirty-two years."

"Long time."

"Damn right."

"What happened to the other tenants?"

"Got relocated. Pushed out was more like it. Maybe about six years ago."

"All but you?"

"I *wouldn't* go." The old geezer flashed his gums at Block in what was meant to be a grin. "Developer went broke. Gave up the property. And here I am. Haven't paid rent in five years, how's that?"

"You can help me, Pops," Block said.

"Name's Mophet."

"Sure, Mr. Mophet. I'm looking for a Marty Nash."

The oldster frowned. "Who?"

"Martin Nash. Used to live at this address."

"When's that?"

"Maybe fifteen, twenty years ago."

"Don't recollect no one with that handle. What's he look like?"

Block described the Nash he had known.

"Nope," Mophet said.

"He had a small scar on his chin, a six-edged star. It was very small."

The oldster stared at Block blankly, then grinned. "Shit. Know the fella you mean."

"You do?"

"Damn right. You led me astray, yes sir."

"How?"

"Said he lived here."

"Yes."

"Never did."

"What was he, the janitor?"

"Shit. That fella, he was the goddam *landlord.*"

"You sure?"

"Sure I'm sure. You think I'm simple or something?"

"Perish the thought, Mr. Mophet."

"Can do without your jokes, too, sonny. This Nash, he was the son of a bitch sold this property to the goddam developer."

"Six years ago?"

"That's right."

"Seen him since?"

"Why should I? Told you he sold the place."

"I'm trying to reach him."

"Can't help you there."

"Got any old receipts?"

"For my rent?"

"Uh-huh."

"Suppose so."

"Receipts have an address?"

"I reckon."

"Think you can find one for me?"

"Hell. Want a lot for five bucks, don't you? That old stuff's packed away in a trunk."

Block fished his wallet out of a pocket, came up with another five-spot.

"Think you can go look, maybe?"

The old bird took the fiver. "Guess so."

"Pretty expensive, Pops."

"Mr. Mophet to you, sonny. Good things cost. Know what this flat's worth? Shit, that's what it's worth."

"I'll wait out here."

"Wasn't going to invite you in."

Block cooled his heels, trying not to breathe too deeply. The stench in the hallway was really something.

After a while the oldster returned, a wrinkled, stained piece of paper in his hand. Wordlessly, he thrust it at Block.

Block took it and went away very fast.

He parked his car in the driveway, sat staring at the swanky three-story frame cottage. Not bad. Sally had done all right for herself. The street was tree-lined, the lawns neat and trimmed. Not much traffic, either. He climbed out, took a whiff of the air; he might've been in the country.

Block strolled up the front walk, wondering if anyone would be home. Midday wasn't the best time for unexpected house calls. If Sally held a job, he'd have to come back in the evening. That would put a damper on the expedition for sure. More and more it looked like a wild goose chase. What had seemed obvious in the morgue was cockeyed in daylight. Even the cadaver's scar no longer seemed the right size, or in the right place. He could just hear Ben Cohen when he returned empty-handed. Nora would give him the business, too. So far he hadn't even come up with enough for a short, first-person piece.

The name under the bell said Hastings. He rang it, waited for a moment, raised his hand to ring again. The door opened.

"Yes?"

He wouldn't have recognized her but for the blond hair. She had just put on weight and grown some—grown up, in fact. She wore plenty of makeup, which gave her face a sort of anonymity. Pretty enough, though, in a big-bosomed, wide-hipped way. Her blue housedress was tight in the right places.

"Sally," he said, "I don't know if you remember me, Ross Block?"

She squinted. "I'm sorry, who?"

"We went to the same school. P.S. 67."

That got him nothing.

"We were in old Mr. Brisbain's English class together."

"Yeah?"

"I used to sit in the first row, over by the window."

"You did, huh?" There was no hint of recognition in her eyes. Block began to wonder if somehow he'd made a mistake—although he couldn't for the life of him imagine what it was.

"Sally Niel, right?"

"Sure. Before I got married."

"Fine. You remember a kid named Whitey Kaplan?"

"The guy played all those instruments?"

"That's him. We used to hang out together."

"*Wait* a minute. You the guy who kept getting all those *A*s?"

"Only in English."

She grinned at Block. "*Sure* I know you. Couldn't place the name, is all. Hey, come on in."

"It's been a long time, Sally."

He followed her through a short hallway into the living room.

"Sit down," she said. "Look, can I get you something? Some coffee, maybe?"

"Sure."

Over coffee and cake Block gave her his spiel.

"I'm a reporter now, Sal, for the *Register,* doing a small piece on what school was like—"

"Yeah, but how'd you find me?"

"Washington High. They had your address."

Sally grinned, shook her head. "That beats everything."

"One of your friends snitched. The school sends out questionnaires. Got any good word about school, Sally? It prepared you for a career?"

"Three marriages is what I had. That and a stretch as a secretary in a real estate firm. Let me tell you, that was for the birds."

"Any kids?"

"Uh-uh."

"Planning?"

"Who knows? Charles and I've only been married like six years. Why rush things, right?"

"So what did you learn in school?"

"To watch TV soaps."

"That's all you got out of it, Sal?"

"Yeah. And you can quote me. That and my first husband."

"Who's that?"

"Nick Siscoe. He died."

Block put down his coffee cup. "I'm sorry."

"Oh, that was ages ago. The second guy I hooked up with was a real louse. Heavy drinker, you know; we split about seven years ago. Then I met Charley. And the rest like is history."

Block glanced around the living room. The rug, furniture, drapes all looked expensive. "Charley brings home the bacon?"

"Can't complain. He's in export-import. The McCoy outfit. It's big business."

"Remember a guy called Marty Nash?"

"Sure, Nick's friend."

"I'd like to talk with him, too."

"Yeah?"

"Can't find his address, though."

Sally shrugged. "Haven't laid eyes on him in years."

"Know anyone who might have?"

"Uh-uh."

She couldn't help him with Rothman and Bell, either.

He stood up to go.

"Thanks, Sally. I've enjoyed this."

"Me too. I'm gonna be in the paper?"

"Yep."

She broke into a huge grin. "Whaddya know?"

— CHAPTER —
Nine

The Data Control maties had knocked off at a reasonable hour; the place was empty when we hit the first level.

"We're in luck," I whispered to the girl. We worked our way along the wall, dodging the spotter-eyes.

She shook her head. *"Something is wrong,"* she whispered

into my ear, too low, I hoped, to be picked up by any magneto-ears left on.

"Better spell it out."

She stood motionless.

"Well?"

"It is *too* quiet.".

"Sure it's quiet. They've all gone home.".

"You do not understand."

"Explain it to me. Let's pretend I'm dumb."

"The Overseers are not this humane. There are *always* some maties about. *Someone* should be here."

"Possibly this setup's different. Could be running this joint gets you more points."

"You truly believe that?"

I shrugged. "No." I moved. "Come on. Stick close to the wall. Let's not make it easy for them."

We skirted the door; using it was beginning to seem a bit premature. We made our way to a window; very carefully I peered out.

The first level of the Data Control was elevated, well above the street. I had a pretty good view of the outside. Dusk had crept across the zone. Long, dark shadows lay over ramps, walkways and buildings. Lit street glowers made dim ovals in the half-light. No need to worry about being seen through this window, there was no one out there. In every direction I looked the walks were completely empty.

"National holiday?" I said.

The girl didn't laugh.

"They must be pretty short on Blanks and computer techs to go to all this trouble."

"Perhaps it is a matter of principle?"

"Yeah. They don't like *anyone* to get away. And are willing to pull all the stops just to get them back. You think so?"

"I do not know. It is possible."

"Sure. On the other hand, maybe one of us really *is* important."

"You think it is *I*?"

"I'm not taking any bets, lady, but gladiators are probably a dime a dozen."

"And politicals?"

"Depends on what kind."

I gazed out the window. Far down the main drive, I saw movement: a number of vehicles. They were heading our way. I looked toward the left. The walkway wasn't empty anymore. A group of uniformed men moved along it. I didn't have to wonder where they were bound. The walkway stopped at our doorstep.

"The welcoming committee," I said.

"They move so slowly."

"Those birds don't figure we're here especially, just in the vicinity. They're shaking down the whole area."

"But not the Data Bank?"

I grinned sourly. "Like I said—to frisk it, you've got to know about it first."

"We could hide there."

"Not anymore. When our four playmates turn out to be missing, all hell will break loose."

"Still—"

"Still, nothing. They're probably not the only ones who know. Half a dozen more would be more like it. And even if the others are halfway around this planet, once they wise up, they'll turn up here like nobody's business."

"But we *must* hide somewhere."

I sighed. She wasn't telling me anything I didn't know. Through the window I could see the wrecking crew getting closer. The only thing we had going for us was their thoroughness: they were peeking under every stone. It'd give us more time. *Only, time for what?*

"It's too late to hide," I told the girl. "Not on this world. Once the Overseers put their minds to it, they'll find us no matter where we are. We've got to keep running."

"How?" she said. "We cannot go out there."

"Just possibly there's another way."

"What way?"

"I'm not sure."

"You do not know?"

"Not enough. We better go back, ask the Data Bank."

"*Now?*"

"When else? We're not likely to get another chance, are we?"

We headed down the staircase, on the double.

I tried not to show it, but I wasn't feeling so great. My

high at beating up the four oldsters was wearing thin. The trick with the digger, uniform and computer was starting to seem dumber with each step I took. The Overseers had lots of practice keeping tabs on maties, rounding up strays. It'd take more than my mind-flow and clicks to get us out of here — nothing less than an invading army would do. And there didn't seem to be one handy. By now I was willing to settle for a solitary tank that could help us blast our way free. That seemed to be in short supply too. All I had was the Data Bank and possibly twenty minutes to come up with something bright. I could feel panic nipping at me. Again. I hated the feeling. I was sorry now I'd brought the girl. She'd been right: by the time the Overseers got done with her, there wouldn't be much left.

We hit the oldsters, still stretched out where I'd dropped them. They meant nothing to me — less than nothing — but I wasted a second to see if they were still alive. Each had a pulse, was breathing; alive — if not kicking. Good enough. I straightened up. I'd thought of taking a hostage or two. Or forcing one of them to help us escape. I gave up the thought. The boys outside played rough, had us outnumbered a thousand to one. These oldsters would only get in the way, help trip us up. I moved on.

The Data Bank lit up as we approached. I was beginning to dread that room.

The girl took her seat by the terminal.

"What do I ask?"

I took a deep breath.

And told her.

It was time to quit the building. Another ten minutes would have us rubbing shoulders with the enemy. Peering out the first-level window — a last hurried glance — I could just about make out their faces. Nothing about them I liked.

"Come," the girl said.

She was showing good sense. I came.

We made a detour to the nearest utility bin, only a few steps away. Ignoring the auto-dusters, broom, mops and pails, I helped myself to a couple of more useful items. Then we made tracks.

The back door was locked. Some surprise. That would be

the first thing they'd see to: everything under lock and key all over the area—orders through the viewscreens issued directly to the maties before they took off. The alarm system would be on too. No special trick of memory needed to reach that conclusion. The Data Bank had spilled the beans, told all.

"Let's see the printout," I said.

Silently the girl handed me a diagram; I got down on hands and knees. The fuse box was locked. But the master-key I'd lifted from the utility bin opened it in a jiffy. I removed only one fuse—why be greedy?—the one my print-out said ran the alarm.

We hotfooted it to the window. It rose without a whisper. I slid over the sill, jumped eight feet to the ground. The girl followed, landed in my arms.

From far away I heard the sounds of voices, men and mechs on the move.

"They will be coming from the other direction also," the girl pointed out.

"The sky too if we don't beat it."

I took her hand; we retreated down the alley. Darkness made the going rough, but using the glower I'd taken from the bin would've tipped off the opposition in no time. We tripped along in the dark. The alley didn't look too promising. We were fenced in on both sides by high walls. And the streets which lay ahead or back of us would be crawling with troops.

I glanced over a shoulder. In the Data building—now considerably behind us—lights were snapping on. It wouldn't take them long to figure what was what. The opened window, the silent alarm would be a dead giveaway, a giant finger pointing in our direction, if we were still cooped up in the alley.

I hoped the computer had been up to date.

"Okay," I said, "this is it."

"What is?"

"Watch."

We halted. I had to risk a light. I half covered the glower with my palm, shone it toward the ground.

"Damn," I murmured. I saw nothing of interest.

We moved forward. I kept the light shining, shielding it as best I could.

"We have miscalculated?" the girl asked. She didn't sound very happy.

"Not yet."

"No?"

"I'm playing it by ear."

"Ah," she said, as if she knew what I was talking about. I was starting to wonder myself. If I'd missed it, gone too far in the darkness, we'd have to backtrack, a sure way of landing in the net.

A slice of light caught an edge of plasto-deck. It was barely visible in the pavement. Barely was enough.

"Paydirt," I told her.

"What did you say?"

"Our passport out of here."

"There are times," she said, "I simply cannot understand you."

"Gladiator talk, probably. I'll take lessons later."

A simple screwdriver from the bin—in place of the crowbar I didn't have—helped me pry open the cover disk. We crawled in, replaced it, climbed down a long ladder and hit bottom.

The glower put a circle of light ahead of us. The tunnel stretched into darkness. A lot of wires and pipes around. We trotted alongside them. I kept eyeing our printout. I wasn't sure we were making the right turns. But I had hopes.

The girl asked, "These are the underground tunnels you spoke of?"

I denied it. "Too far away. And by now covered. This is pure improvisation. I almost didn't think of it. And they never will."

"Think of what?" There was a hint of annoyance in her voice.

I grinned. I was almost starting to enjoy myself again. It didn't take much, just a little success.

I said, "We had two choices, both underground."

"Two."

"Right. The waste and drainage system was one. You wouldn't like it. Too smelly."

"Smelly?"

"Yeah. And wet, slippery. It'd've been lousy going from the start."

"Lousy going?"

"Sure. And the nearest cover disk was out on the street. Scratching that angle for keeps."

"*So where are we?*"

"The utilities belt. Stretches under the whole sector. Clean, too. All we got to do is keep from getting lost."

"And they will not look here?"

"Not for a while."

"Why?"

"No way for us to find this place, let alone get around in it. They'll figure we went to Data Control, hunting maps, checkpoints, transit routes. All classified. So we moved on empty-handed through the window. And are lying low somewhere in the zone. Simple."

"The alarm signal."

"What about it?"

"They will wonder how we knew to disarm it."

"Yeah, that'll give 'em something to think about. So what? They won't know about the Data Bank; that'll take time. And time is what we need."

We rested after a while, stretched out on the plasto-deck floor. No sound except our breathing. I kept the glower on: its light made our environment seem less dreary. Black night rolled in on us from both ends of the tunnel, washed over everything. I liked the darkness too, the quiet. As long as it lasted, no one could nab us. I closed my eyes. I must've dozed. The dream came again, the one I'd been having over and over.

The Palace of Light glittered all around me. It was clearer this time than it had ever been before. The haze was there as always, but now it seemed less substantial. I saw the towers through the curtained windows and knew that they were part of a vast city. I turned my attention to the man. He surprised me. I had thought him middle-sized. But now I saw he was quite short. His head was round, his body rotund. He had blond curly hair, sharp blue eyes, a wide nose and full lips. He was in his mid-fifties, I knew, but looked younger. The others around him, previously dim figures, now acquired character. The one who hovered at the short man's elbow was slender, long-faced, with thin lips, a flat nose. He whispered into the blond man's ear. The other figure on the far right was equally distinct. He appeared to be in his late sixties, was of medium height, with brown glistening eyes, black hair. His shoulders seemed too large for his squarish body. He kept rubbing his hands together and smiling. I glanced around at the other faces. They bobbed and weaved before me. They did not seem as important as these other two. Or the short blond man around whom everything seemed to revolve.

This time, I felt certain I would discover his identity. It was only a matter of moving closer, of making sense of the words these people spoke. Already I seemed to be on the verge of some incredible understanding which would put all my speculations to rest.

But I had forgotten the tall figure by the door.

He moved, and the darkness came with him. He was a blur of motion.

Heads whirled to face him. Figures lost their solidity. Floor, ceiling and walls seemed to merge, become one, at once opaque and transparent.

The distant towers poked their long points through the room, splintering it. I caught a glimpse of the streets beyond. There were many sections, some built according to plan, others haphazard and misshapen. The sections folded in on themselves. Masses of people raced along the pavements. They were swallowed up as the concrete cracked open.

The small blond man opened his full lips and screamed. He began to crumble like a plaster figure.

The tall dark man shattered like a glass statue.

The lights were blinking out.

I made one last effort to hold the scene together, to put back the smashed pieces. I had been only a step away from ultimate knowledge.

I saw the girl then—for the very first time. She had long blond hair, deep-green eyes. And she was screaming.

The sight of the girl was too much for me. I lost control of the image. I was screaming too. I plunged into a deep black pit. It closed over me. I was gone.

I opened my eyes slowly.

I don't know where the hell I expected to be, but the utility belt wasn't one of the places. I noticed two things right off: I was soaked through with sweat, and the girl was shaking me.

"Yeah . . ." I managed to mumble.

"You were screaming."

I sat up, put my back against the wall, took a couple of deep breaths. "How long was I out?"

"Twenty minutes perhaps."

"I had this damn dream."

"Yes?"

"You were in it."

She nodded. "That is only natural—under these circumstances."

"You were screaming. The world was breaking up."

"It is," she said. "For us."

"Not that way. It was coming apart like in an explosion. I've had this dream before."

She smiled. "And I was always in it?"

"This is the first time."

"You see?"

"The first couple of times it was always hazy, out of whack."

"But now?"

"It's grown clearer."

"And you think this important?"

"I don't know. It might be a clue to the past, something the Overseers forgot to erase. You could have been in it all along and I just noticed. Could be that's why you looked so familiar when I first saw you."

"Yes, perhaps."

"All this stuff I know, the little and big secrets that just pop into my head—it's got to come from *somewhere.*"

Her face was earnest. "I have no memory of my past."

"Possibly this will help. My dream takes place in some kind of palace."

"How do you know that?"

"A guess. There's a city outside with great big towers. Ring a bell?"

She shrugged, shook her head.

"Yeah," I said bitterly, "the Overseers do a dandy job, don't they?"

"Only to those who have committed a *terrible* crime."

"Don't bet on it. There's a tall, thin man in this dream with thin lips and a flat nose. And a squarish one with broad shoulders who keeps smiling. Anyone you might know?"

"No."

"How about a little fat guy with blond curly hair? He's got blue eyes, thickish lips, a wide nose. And as far as I can tell, he's the boss."

"No." She sounded hesitant.

"Nothing at all? *Think!*"

"Nothing."

"But *something* happened with you just now."

"Yes."

"What was it?"

She shuddered. "I do not know. But I am suddenly very *afraid.*"

— CHAPTER —

Ten

Block's drive to Manhattan took him past P.S. 67 again. Late afternoon. The schoolyard was crowded with kids. He slowed, gave them the once-over, searching for someone who might have been him. No soap. The long-ago Ross Block was nowhere in sight. Even the mode of dress was different. He turned a corner and left the school behind.

Block sighed. His trip to yesteryear had turned up no scoops but had left him strangely dissatisfied. Too many changes had all but erased his past, torn up whatever roots he had in these streets.

He turned left for two blocks, then right for three more. He pulled up at the curb and got out. Where the five-story tenement he'd called home in the fifties used to be, only weeds now grew. All the buildings had come down. Nothing had gone up. He stared at the general emptiness, shrugged. He didn't return to the car. He hiked down a block, turned west, and hit a small shopping section. He walked along slowly, hands stuffed in pockets, looking left and right.

The pair of supermarkets were new. But he remembered

the corner gas station. The guy inside the candy store was Spanish. In Block's day Schwartz had run the place—a wonderland of candy, ice cream and comic books. The old guy had called all the kids by name, too. Block shook his head, moved on. The cleaning store was still there, a couple of doors away, but the folks holding down the counter were both Oriental. Block didn't recall the locksmith or the TV repair shop. The ice cream parlor looked to be brand-new. The kosher butcher was gone, his place taken by a fruit and vegetable store.

It occurred to Block that this sightseeing was a sure sign that he'd lost his marbles. Ben Cohen would pull the rug out from under him if he didn't show anything for his efforts. But instead of hustling he was mooning around his old neighborhood, peering through store windows, hunting for a trace of the world he'd once done his best to escape from. He was cracked.

He'd reached the last block, before stores gave way to projects. He passed a used-furniture store, a card shop, a Spanish grocery. And stopped short. The weathered sign across the street read Lefkowitz's Shoe Repair. The old guy and Block had been buddies; he'd dropped in every once in a while just to chat. Lefky would be pushing eighty—if he was still kicking around, which wasn't any too likely. But someone had saved his sign.

Block crossed over against the traffic.

The man inside still had a full head of white hair. He wore thick glasses. His forehead and cheeks were creased and wrinkled. But he was only a little more stooped than when Block had known him. He opened the door, went in.

"Lefky?"

The old man looked up. "Yes?"

"It's me," Block said, a bit in shock.

"Which me?"

"Ross Block."

"Rossy?"

Block grinned, nodded; he was a kid again, too shy to speak.

He thrust an arm across the counter. They shook hands long and hard. The old man still had a grip of iron.

"Lefky, what are you doing here?"

"Where should I be?"

"Retired?"

"That's all I need. What would I be doing, playing gin rummy in an old-age home? Listen, you got a few minutes? We go next door, have a cup of coffee. There we talk."

It was fine with Block.

"So, your parents?"

"Gone," Block said.

"Also mine wife, Bessie. Twelve years ago."

"The children?"

"Thank God, Judy is married to a physics professor. They are in California. I am a grandfather, two boys, Stephen and Ira. Morris, my youngest, is also married. He is in the clothing business in New Jersey. From him, one granddaughter, Myra. Them I see once a month. California is already too far to go. And you, Rossy, are by now married, of course."

"Not of course."

"So what are you waiting for? You think maybe you are growing younger?"

"I keep hoping."

"Good luck. And your business?"

"That's what brings me here, Lefky. I'm a reporter."

"Ah-ho. All those books you read—they came to something, eh? For what paper?"

"The *Register*."

"*Nu*, so long you are making a living, who can complain?"

"Yeah, that's how I feel about it. *Almost*. Look, I'm doing a piece on the old neighborhood."

"Schwartz and me was all that was left. Now just me. Schwartz, may he rest in peace, has been gone eight years. A good man; also a good provider for his family."

"Lefky, remember Howard Bell, Bernie Rothman?"

"Why not? Bernie, he moved away, a little after you, Rossy; I don't know where to."

"Scratch Bernie. What about Bell?"

Lefky took a sip of coffee, a bite of cake. "He is dead, Rossy."

"Jesus, another one. How?"

"The war."

"Vietnam?"

Lefky nodded.

Block sighed, sat back. "I sure picked a fine bunch for my piece. Remember Nick Siscoe? He was killed in an auto accident. If I had time I'd go back and start over."

Lefky shrugged. "So make time."

Block spooned some pea soup into his mouth. "This story was my idea. If I don't come up with something in a day or so, the whole thing's kaput. But darned if I even remember most of the kids I went to school with."

"Senility, *nabach,* in one so young."

"Wise guy. What makes you think I hung out in public schools when I was a kid? Before my pa went broke, I went to a private school. Classy, eh?"

"This I never knew."

"Sure. Only the best for little Rossy. I spent maybe two and a half years in 67. The kids I really knew were the ball-players. And I never went to Washington High, either. Parents moved right about then. See what I'm up against?"

"Maybe then you should not do this story, ah? Not that you need such suggestions from me."

"I can use all the help I can get, Lefky. Thing is, I'm not really interested in those kids. Just one guy in particular."

"So?"

"Marty Nash."

"Ah-ha."

"Keep it under your hat. I'm trying to run the guy down— so far nothing. On the other hand, so far hasn't been all that long."

"About this Marty Nash, maybe *I* can tell you a thing or two."

"You *can?*"

"From what I have heard. Not, of course, from personal knowledge."

"The guy's a celebrity?"

"He is not a nice man, this Nash; long ago there was talk. It was so bad I still remember."

"I'm all ears. What did he do, stick up a candy store?"

"You are close, Rossy."

"I was kidding."

"He was in what they call loansharking."

"The real stuff, or just penny-ante?"

"This I do not know. But he lent a *lot* of money. And if you were, God forbid, late in paying back, then it was *very* bad for you."

"Meaning what?"

"They broke Mr. Morgan's arm."

"The big Irish guy, the one who ran the bar?"

"That is right, Rossy."

"Jesus. Morgan used to be a boxer."

"Ah-ha."

"*Who* broke his arm? Not Nash?"

"That would be silly; Mr. Nash was the *boss.* Why would he dirty his hands?"

"Yes. And Morgan would've killed him."

"Three men it was. At night when Mr. Morgan closes."

"That's about two A.M."

"Yes. They fell on him with sticks, with baseball bats."

"How was Nash tied to it?"

"Everybody knew. Mr. Nash made no secret of it. The next day he was in the neighborhood boasting."

"Had a lot of clients, I bet."

Lefky nodded. "He wanted them to know: no monkey business."

"And that did the trick?"

"I'll tell you, Rossy, you paid interest every week and it was sky-high."

"It's called the vig."

"Ah-ha. Well, some, they just could not pay. They had bad luck. Or maybe business was bad."

"Nash call in the goon squad again?"

"Twice. Mrs. Grossberg owed him."

"The grocery lady?"

"That is right."

"Jesus. He had an old woman beat up?"

"Her son."

"Danny?"

"Danny."

"He was just a kid."

"Maybe sixteen. Two weeks he was in the hospital."

"Grossberg pay then?"

"How could she pay? There was no money."

"What happened?"

"She gave him the store."

"Just like that?"

"Sure. *Three* other stores he got, too. And when Schultz, the dairyman, wouldn't give him *his* store, he was shot."

"Killed?"

"No, thank God; Schultz was in the hospital for maybe three weeks. From his hospital bed, Rossy, he sold his dairy to a chain. You hear?"

"Yes. He pulled a fast one on old Nash."

"And how! He moved to Florida the same day he left the hospital."

"Smart cooky. Sounds like half the neighborhood was in hock to Nash. Didn't they believe in banks?"

"My dear young man, what can I tell you? This was when? In the sixties sometime, ah? Here was a poor neighborhood. Times were not good. Who went to banks? Sure, when people saw what was happening, then they said goodbye to Mr. Nash. No one would do business with him. Only then, for a lot, it was already too late. They were finished. That is the way it goes."

"What became of Nash?"

"Who knows? The stores he got, he sold again right away. The money which we owed him, I am sure he somehow collected in full. And he himself, what should a man like that do? He is beating people somewhere else."

"But you have no idea where?"

Lefky smiled. "I have not even heard the name Marty Nash in fifteen years."

"That's some story, Lefky."

"You like it, ah?"

"It's what I was looking for."

"So I was some help?"

"I'll say. And seeing you, Lefky, has been the high point of my day."

"The feeling is mutual."

"Make that month. Even year."

"You were always a little bit of a faker, Rossy."

"So who's perfect?"

"You will do me a favor?"

"Don't even ask. This bill's on me. Go on, have a second cup of coffee, even. All that stuff about my being tight is just stuff. Prudent maybe—"

"Be quiet, Rossy."

"Yes sir, my lips are sealed."

"I want you to promise me you will come back, and tell to me the end of this. I have your word?"

Block raised his hand. "Scout's honor."

"All right, then; because you are such a good boy, I tell you one more thing."

"There's something else?"

"A little. And I make you a gift of it."

"That's smart," Block said in his Humphrey Bogart voice. "You don't want to hold out on Little Rossy."

"God forbid. Little Rossy, ah? What are you, a smart aleck? Listen. This Nick Siscoe you mentioned. The one which was killed in the accident."

"What about him?"

"It was said he was a silent partner of Mr. Nash."

— CHAPTER —
Eleven

The night was black.

I replaced the cover disk, took the girl's hand and moved to the even blacker shadows of an adjacent building.

No one out on the streets. Only the sound of the wind gusting over the pavements.

"Not bad," I told the girl.

"Where are we?"

"On our way out."

I steered her along the wall, across to the next building. Still too soon to pat myself on the back, but I was beginning to think I'd pulled it off. Gotten us through the utility belt to the right spot.

I peered around the wall.

Before us was a dark, level plain. Only one structure broke the smoothness of the horizon. It was dimly lit and about a quarter link away.

"That's it," I said.

"*It* being what?" the girl asked in her husky voice.

"The engine unit."

"We are about to steal an engine?"

"That's the idea."

"They will let us?"

"They won't have anything to say about it, but they'll squawk plenty later."

We moved out onto the plain. Dark earth crunched underfoot. I kept looking around for any spectators to our little jaunt; there were none.

"Nice, secluded place, isn't it?"

"It feels so strange. I am unused to being alone."

"You're not alone. You've got me for company."

"But it is desolate here."

"Right. What did you expect, a crowd? That's all we need."

We trudged on in silence. The girl had a point. None of this felt right. I'd gone out on some forays before. And my biggest battle was fighting panic. Outside of the work zones, the prison compound, I was a total stranger. I knew there were hundreds of worlds out there, gigantic cities, forests, oceans: all that had clicked into place. But none of those things mattered for me. I *felt* like a Blank. And every step of the way I had to fight that feeling. What must the girl be going through? What memories did she have to fall back on? At least I'd been planning something like this all along. But for her, it had come out of nowhere. That she wasn't in shock, that she'd hung in there with me every step of the way, was a cockeyed wonder.

I reached out, took her hand. It felt cold and moist in my grip. I still had the feeling that I'd known her somewhere before. I thought back to the dream, the one in which she'd been screaming. I could see her clear as day in my mind's eye.

I said, "They let you keep any of your clothes?"

"None. It is against regulations. We *all* must wear the uniform."

"Yeah, mustn't we? Does a dark-blue blouse with a very wide collar mean anything to you?"

"Should it?"

"You had it on in the dream."

"That *again?*" She smiled.

"I'm a crank. How about this: a long, light-blue skirt with lots of pleats."

"I was wearing this too?"

"Who else?"

"I have no memory of such a garment. Was I elegant?"

"You were a peach." I tried to focus on the dream. She'd been screaming, lips drawn back from white teeth, eyes wide, neck muscles straining. Her hand went up to her mouth. I saw something else.

"You had on earrings."

"Earrings?"

"Yeah. Shaped like small shells."

"This concept *earrings*, for a mere instant, it was unknown to me."

"You caught on, though?"

"Yes."

"But never wore any?"

"No."

"That's what I figured."

We continued in silence again. The engine unit was growing closer. I thought of all the ground we still had to cover — even if we laid our hands on some kind of craft. The thought didn't do much to cheer me.

"You had a ring on," I said.

"A ring?"

"Yeah, a ring. On your right hand. Had three small stones on a silver band."

I felt her hand grow cold in mine; it was like ice.

"I once had such a ring."

"*Where? When?*"

"They took it away. It was precious to me. I had it only for a short while."

"Why did they let you keep it?"

"I do not know. An oversight; perhaps it was difficult to remove."

"Yeah. Or maybe you were just too much somebody to monkey with."

It was a short, squat structure that made up in length and width what it lacked in height. There were no windows, but a number of doors, all probably locked.

The girl whispered. "There are guards?" She huddled

close to me, against the wind. I had my arm around her. I felt faint stirrings that had long been forgotten, that had, in fact, all but slipped my mind. I was beginning to dislike the Overseers more than ever.

"There shouldn't be any," I said.

"The maps do not tell?"

"Not a word."

"Then how can you be sure?"

"Because I've been here."

"They *let* you?"

"They *made* me. I helped build this place. Me and my digger. Usually I never got to see the finished product. But they needed some extra holes and I got a good look at the unit when it was already up."

"You knew yourself then?"

"More or less."

"My co-workers know where they came from—and even I knew of outside worlds—yet none of them ever sought to escape."

"Yeah, where would they go? And how? They'd have run into a stone wall trying. That's where I've got the edge. I wanted to get out and I started remembering how to do it. Possibly I used to be a guard once. Or maybe I helped build prisons. Whatever it was, it's worked so far. Let's see if there've been any changes since my last visit."

I guided her away from the building.

"You had *planned* to come back?" she said.

"I'd planned nothing. I tried to leave a little something at each site I worked. In case I *did* come back, I stole things. Uniforms, tools, code keys. Anything and everything I thought might come in handy. And I hid it. No one paid any attention to a Blank."

"And you never marveled at your initiative?"

"That's *all* I thought about, but I didn't come up with any big answers. I didn't come up with any answers at all."

I drew to a halt.

We had been moving east, away from the structure. This looked to be about the right spot.

I shone my light down on the ground. Anyone around would be able to see it. I was betting there was no one around. The circle of light grew larger as I swung it back and forth. It took a while to find what I was looking for.

Only the tip of the large stone was still visible. The three smaller stones were buried in the dirt. I kicked away the top layer, and there they were. A couple of weeks more and I'd've blown the whole operation: all my careful markings would have been buried by the wind.

The four stones made a straight line. I moved right, extending the line by ten steps.

The girl held the glower. I got down on hands and knees, used the screwdriver to dig up my package.

We headed back to the engine unit. In my hand I carried a small plastic bag. It contained only a few items. I hoped they would do the trick.

I circled the unit trying doors. I had the code key in my hand, the one I'd lifted long ago and buried in my plastic bag. It was going to be a snap. Especially if they hadn't changed the code. But then why should they?

The sixth door I came to clicked open when I inserted the key. The magnetic code doused the alarm; we stepped into a dark interior. The unmistakable odors of an engine unit came to me: oil, rubber, plasto-deck, power packs, quick-gleam polish. I played my glower over rows and rows of assorted vehicles.

"You can drive them?" the girl asked.

"Sure. If I can drive a digger, I can drive one of these. Besides, it seems to be a skill that's clicked back into place. At least some of it."

We started down an aisle, my light flicking over at least a dozen different drive-mechs. A couple were meant for air travel. They got my special attention.

"What do you think?" the girl asked.

"Looks like we've got our pick. I'll know more when I take a gander at the controls."

"And fuel?"

"Most've got power packs. They're probably charged up. If not, we can charge 'em ourselves. That's why I chose this place. It's got possibilities."

I steered her over to a hovercraft.

"We could do worse than this baby," I said.

The girl looked doubtful. "It is not very large."

"Yeah. Just a tiny two-seater. Skims over the ground but

can hit the heights, too. That's important. We've got a ways to go. On a dark night you can hardly see it. That's a plus. Our pals the Overseers have lots of gadgets set up to spot ground cars. Same goes for aircraft. Not that we wouldn't have a fighting chance. There are ways to avoid spotter-eyes, detector beams. And I even know some of them. At least *I think* I do. But with this baby we can forget all that. It flies too high to bump into the ground systems and too low for air surveillance systems. It's where the Overseers slipped up. And it's what I've been counting on."

The girl was looking at me strangely.

"Something the matter?"

She hesitated. "The way you sound."

"What about it?"

"You appear so—*certain.*"

"Don't worry," I told her, "I'll probably get over it real soon."

I crawled into the hovercraft and gave it a look-see. Reaching into my plastic bag, I felt around for the code key. My hand came out with half a dozen. I chose the long, flat key, stuck it in the lock, heard it click into place. Nothing happened. I crawled out again.

"It does not function?"

"Power pack may be out. Let's hope so."

I went around to the back of the craft. The engine panel was locked. The keys would be somewhere at the unit's far end, in the storage tube. It wasn't worth the trip. I used the screwdriver on the panel. It popped open without much effort. The panel was empty.

"Nothing comes easy," I told the girl.

There were two other hovercrafts. Neither had a power pack.

I sighed. "Let's go," I said.

We trekked around the engine unit a good ten minutes before we found the storage tube. Like everything else in the place, it was locked. No code slot fit over the keyhole. A simple padlock held the round door in place.

I put the screwdriver to work again. Next to the girl, it was becoming my most useful item. I congratulated myself on having the good sense to bring both on this expedition.

The screw eyes proved a tougher nut to crack than the

engine panel, but a little elbow grease did the trick. The lock fell to the floor. I pushed the door open, shone my light inside.

Behind me the girl gasped.

She had good reason.

The power packs were all lined up in neat rows on the shelves, just there for the taking.

Only we'd never reach them.

A large, ugly robot stood in the way. His tiny red eye cells seemed to be glaring at us reproachfully. Or possibly my conscience was starting to bother me.

The robot spoke:

"Identify yourselves."

That's all we needed.

I stared at the robot. The robot stared back at me. I didn't like it one bit.

"Identify yourselves," the robot demanded again. "Produce your authorization at once!"

I searched my mind for the word or phrase that would calm this metal watchdog; my mind refused to cooperate.

The silence was unnerving. I was actually becoming embarrassed.

The robot broke the spell.

His arms went wide as though he were about to embrace us.

He took a ponderous step forward.

"It is my duty to restrain you," he intoned. "Unless you choose to identify yourselves."

This robot had a one-track mind.

He took another step toward us. "You have been warned."

The girl's voice came from behind me. "He is slow. We could run."

I backed up a step. "I don't think so," I said. "Where would we go? We've got to get around this thing. Stay behind me. Back up slowly."

"Halt!" the robot said. He took another step in our direction. I could see this chase going on till morning. I didn't have till morning.

"It is not a security robot," the girl said.

"We'd be behind bars if it was," I said.

"Halt!" the robot said.

"What is it then?"

"Maintenance robot, I'd guess."

"Halt!"

"Just doing its duty. Like it said."

"Halt!"

By now we were back in the unit proper. The robot kept coming. He'd never catch up, just louse up our escape.

"Halt!"

The robot lunged forward.

I didn't back up. This time I went to meet him.

His arms began to close around me.

I smelled oil, quick-gleam polish, plasto-deck cleanser.

The girl let out a yell.

I still had the screwdriver in my hand. I plunged it into the robot's left eyesocket.

Sparks.

Crackling sounds.

Smoke.

I stepped back, dropped the screwdriver. I'd gotten a shock.

It was worth it.

The robot stood stock still, its arms out as if it were about to sing a popular tune. No lights shone from either the whole or the ruined eyesocket. The robot had as much life in it as any thumbtack. And about as much personality.

"That's that," I said.

"I feared it had caught you."

"Not a chance."

"You guessed the robot would cease to function?"

"Yeah."

"But *how?*"

I shrugged. "Comes from knowing the ropes."

"Your abilities are so *strange.*"

"Lady, just being on this world is strange."

She touched my arm. There was awe in her voice. "You possess *vast* internal resources."

"Thanks. Just keep praying they don't go on the blink."

"What is next?"

"The power pack. And hovercraft."

"And then?"

"We take a ride."

Block used a pay phone, fed it a dime, dialed the *Register's* number, asked for Ben Cohen and waited till a familiar voice came on the line.

"Yeah?"

"Ross here."

"Where's here?"

"Brooklyn."

"Christ, son, we haven't run a piece on Brooklyn in four months, maybe five."

"More like a year."

"That's right. So stop wasting the paper's money and come home. Hell, if I'd known this great mysterious story of yours was in *Brooklyn*, I'd've nixed the whole thing. You *are* there on this John Doe business, and not just hanging around?"

"John Doe."

"Okay, so I can't fire you. But I can pull you off this nonsense. And I will, too. You got one more day, Ross— make it a good one. Christ, Brooklyn, of all things."

"You done yet?"

"Sure. I'm a busy man, can't go on bullshitting all day. What's up?"

"Gotta see you."

"Yeah?"

"Story's starting to break—we should talk."

"Fine with me. Said so all along. How about tomorrow?"

"Uh-uh. I want to get an early start. I'll be back in the city about six. Think you can meet me at Maxy's?"

"Only if the drinks are on you."

"It's a deal."

"Sucker."

"Over here, Ross."

Cohen was seated at a small corner table, nursing a gin

and tonic, his usual. The place was crowded. Block side-stepped a waiter, a pair of customers, pulled out a chair and joined the editor.

Cohen drained his glass, signaled the waiter. "Another for me. And some white wine for my friend." He turned to Block. "You look beat."

"It's been one rough day, Ben."

"Eaten?"

"Cake, lots of coffee. A bowl of soup. On the whole, no."

"Chow's not half bad here. Let's have dinner. You really got something?"

"Hope so."

"Okay." Cohen slapped the table, making their drinks jump. "On the expense account!"

"Just my luck," Block complained. "You foot the bill and I pick Maxy's."

"After this piece of yours doubles circulation," Cohen grinned, "I take you to the Ritz."

Over a steak dinner Block filled Cohen in.

"A scar, you say?" Cohen said when Block was done.

"A scar. But not just any scar."

"Very thin stuff, Ross."

"It's Marty, believe me."

"Okay, say it is. Then what?"

"Remember, Ben, I've just begun."

"Yeah. Steak okay?"

"Great. Marty loansharked, right?"

"Back when. Ancient history."

"Uh-huh. But not quite a nickel-and-dime operation."

"So?"

"Connections."

"Tell me why."

"Funding. Where does Marty, a two-bit punk, come up with dough for all this?"

"Your Nick Siscoe?"

"Maybe. It'd take plenty, though. My guess is, more than Siscoe had. And to set up shop like that in any district would call for the mob's say-so."

"So your pal Nash had an in with the mob."

"That's what I'm betting on. Right at the start of his career, let's say. But who knows how far up the ladder he went?"

"Maybe he didn't."

"Uh-huh. So how come they chopped him up? Would some goon rate that much attention?"

"Depends on the circumstances."

"Listen, Ben, Marty was fixed so no one could ID him; why?"

"You tell me."

"If you knew *who* he was you could probably come up with *why* he died, and who bumped him off."

"Christ, what a brainstorm. How come you're so smart?"

"Read the right comic books. Never fails. It makes sense, Ben. Sure, we're still missing most of the pieces—"

"*That* is the understatement of the year."

"Maybe. But we've got the big piece, the one they want hushed up."

"*They.*"

"With it we can blow the lid off their operation."

"Operation, huh?"

Block pushed away his plate. "You're right, food's fine. Should've eaten here before. What's for dessert?"

"Stay away from the coconut cream pie."

"No good?"

"Too good. You'll overeat."

They both had the pie and a couple of coffees to wash it down. Cohen lit a cigar. "Can't say the paper doesn't treat you right, son. Feast fit for a king. Even when you bring me goofy stories."

"Goofy? We'll see about that."

"Yeah, we will. I'm giving you the green light on this. Not that I'm convinced."

"Course not."

"'It's wild conjecture, Ross. When you and Nash had that fight, how old were you?"

"Twelve."

"And you're positive—absolutely sure—that that's the scar?"

Block nodded. "No doubt about it."

"Nuts. With a memory like that you ought to be on the stage: the Great Blockhead, memory whiz. You're wasting your goddam precious talent."

"The trouble with you, Ben, is you're too old."

"That's the trouble, all right."

"You don't remember what it's like being a kid."

"Sometimes I can't even remember my phone number."

"Listen. Nash and I made up. We played ball together. I got to see that scar—and the one on his chin, too—maybe five, six times."

"Sure, a whole lot."

"Uh-huh. But that's not why I remember it. It's the *ring*, Ben. You had to send away for it, see? Took six boxtops of Kix plus a buck seventy-five. That's expensive for a kid. But worth every penny. The ring glowed in the dark. It had a magic decoder built into it. You could flash signals with it, too. And wearing it made you an official Junior Crime Buster. Most kid's rings were plastic. But this one was part metal."

Ben Cohen grinned at Block good-naturedly, took a puff of his cigar. "Before, Ross, I just *thought* you were crazy; now I know it for sure."

"Yeah, yeah. You just don't understand what being a Junior Crime Buster meant. There were all kinds of official documents you had to sign."

"Sign."

"Sure. With the ring. The metal six-edged star of the ring. If I've seen that mark once, I've seen it a hundred times."

"Not a thousand?"

"I had a short attention span as a kid."

Cohen sighed. "All right. Let's say the guy is definitely Marty Nash."

"Now you're talking."

"Let's say he stayed in the rackets, worked his way up. Maybe even became a big shot. But he rubbed someone the wrong way, or made some kind of boo-boo so the mob figured it had to get rid of him. How am I doing?"

"Perfect."

"All right. Now let's say that the guy who makes Nash can blow the whole racket sky-high."

"Hell, Ben, and I thought you'd never understand."

"Oh, I get it, all right. What's not to get? But to find out what Nash was up to, you're to go poking around all over the joint, right?"

"Right."

"Won't take the opposition long to figure out what you're doing."

"I guess not."

"I mean, no way to *mask* it, they'll *know*."

"Uh-huh."

"So tell me something."

"Sure."

"How you figure on staying alive?"

— CHAPTER —
THIRTEEN

We headed south.

The dark countryside swept by below us. Overhead, distant stars twinkled at each other cheerfully. Good cheer ended right there.

My hands felt cold and sweaty on the control lever. My mouth was dry, like a parched desert, and my forehead wet. I kept fighting the urge to ask the girl to take over.

I peered out the cockpit window. There was only darkness.

I looked back at the control panel. I didn't like what I saw.

I began to wonder how I'd gotten off the ground. And what I had to do to get back on it.

The girl put her hand on mine. "You are concerned over something?"

"Hysterical's more like it." My voice sounded hoarse and raspy, as though I'd spent the last hour screaming. "I can't seem to remember how to fly this thing."

I grinned at the girl, trying to put hope and encouragement in my grin. I didn't quite make it. Her face drained of color.

"But you knew before."

"I *thought* I did."

"What happened?"

"I lost it."

The girl's hand went to the control stick. "This holds us steady?"

"Yeah."

"I will guide the craft."

"Great."

"Close your eyes. Lean back and think of the craft. It will come to you."

"*You sure?*"

"But it must."

She was right. We'd run out of alternatives.

I let go of the lever, took a deep breath, leaned back in my chair and tried to relax. It wasn't easy. I told the girl: "Keep an eye out for enemy craft. That lever steers her. The red knob gives you power. If we get company, move away from it as fast as you can. Got that?"

The girl nodded. "What is it you do not remember about flying?"

"All the rest of it."

I closed my eyes.

I could hear the motor's hum, feel its vibrations go through me. I tried to think of the hovercraft, draw a bead on it. But the purring engine lulled me. I took another long breath, sank deeper into the seat. I felt as if I were back on my digger, its energy part of me. My mind could trace its wires, circuits, follow the energy waves as they left my body, flowed into the machine. I sighed peacefully. It was clear as day. The digger was one of the Arm's simpler creations. I could have constructed one myself if I had the parts.

The digger, which had by now turned into an elaborate diagram in my mind, began to fade out. The scene shifted to my dream. Only it wasn't my dream at all, but something else.

I saw a narrow, white-walled, windowless room. The small chubby blond-haired man was there. He wore a metal cap on his head which was attached by an insulated wire to a square black box that half protruded from the wall. His eyes were closed. Was he asleep, dead? I didn't know. The room began to spin around and around. I could hear a loud voice speaking, but I couldn't tell where it was coming from or understand the words.

The scene went blank.

I was in the hovercraft, seated in the cockpit. But at the same time I was part of the craft itself. The merging of myself with the airship surprised me. I hadn't realized the craft was a cyborg too. Now my job was easier. I swept down through the control panel, into the ship's engine. I raced back and forth along the wiring, tracing the energy patterns. A diagram began to take shape in my mind. The hovercraft was an even simpler machine than the digger. I wondered why I hadn't seen that before.

Then I was back in the white-walled room. The short man was still on his cot, motionless. But the voice had grown louder, shriller. The voice seemed to be coming from the walls themselves. I had to leave this room. I spied the door then, in the far corner. I sprang for it, twisted the knob. I was running down a dark, narrow corridor. The voice behind me had begun to scream. I raced on ahead. The door I came to was half ajar; pale light spilled into the darkness. I ran through. The girl was there and she was screaming, too. The floor opened up and I plunged down. I fell head over heels into darkness.

The girl was shaking me. I opened my eyes; they felt as though I had lead weights on them. I shook my head, tried to throw off the drowsiness.

"Look," the girl said.

I looked.

In the distance, thousands of lights glowed below us, stretched for vast links. A city. I didn't know which one.

"We must avoid it," the girl said.

I nodded. I was almost too groggy to speak.

The girl looked at me intently. "Our destination," she said. "You have not told me how to reach it. Do we head east or west?"

A good question, one I'd been asking myself all along.

I focused hazily on the control panel. It was a blur of dials, gauges, levers and knobs. I blinked away the haziness, looked again.

I moved my right hand, turned a yellow knob two notches to the left. A map sprang up on the nine-inch viewscreen. I depressed the red button. A red dot appeared on the map.

The dot was our hovercraft. Next I gave the keyboard my attention, punched out Sector Fourteen and its co-ords. A green-and-gold circle materialized on the map, marking, respectively, our departure and destination points. I turned the black dial from manual to autopilot. The computer brain would automatically transfer the necessary data to the autopilot. And the hovercraft would take it from there. Easy as pie.

I sat back in my seat, carefully examined my handiwork. Nothing to complain about. I felt the craft slowly change course. I turned to the girl. "We head west," I said.

"You know how to fly it now."

"It knows how to fly itself. And I know what to tell it so that it'll go to the right place."

"This knowledge was in your mind?"

"Yeah. Although it sure didn't sound like it was coming from me."

"And you used the method which I suggested to retrieve this knowledge?"

"Something along those lines."

"What do you mean?"

"I started out that way. But I got sidetracked."

"How?"

"You remember the dream I told you about?"

"Of course."

"It came back—in part. And you were in it, again."

"I?"

"Yeah. You and the small fat man. Only the setting was different. You were both in different rooms. I ran down a long corridor. You were in the last room. You were screaming. Then I was falling into darkness. Screwy, huh?"

"That was your dream?"

"Want more? The little man was on a cot, he wore a metal skullcap. A wire ran back to a machine stuck in the wall. He might've been dead or taking a snooze. You were on your feet. There was a voice yammering away in the background. It was just gibberish to me."

"And you were still in the same city as before?"

"Could be. But all I got to see of it this time was the pair of white rooms."

The girl was silent for a moment. "I have seen such a room."

"Yeah? Where?"

"Here. We were shown it."

"What was it?"

"The erasure chamber. I have told you, the others with whom I worked knew more of their past than I. Most had never been subjected to the erasure. They were a privileged class."

"Lucky them."

"My office zone was given a tour of punitive chambers. I was permitted to attend."

"Sounds like fun. What did they show you, how to put on thumbscrews?"

"We were taken by ground car to a penal colony. Perhaps it was yours?"

"Or someone else's. It hardly matters. The one thing they've got plenty of around here is penal colonies. That's when you saw the white room?"

"The erasure chamber, yes."

"What else was in it?" I wanted to know.

"Nothing."

"You sure?"

The girl nodded. "It was precisely as you described it. Neither more nor less."

"Okay, that clears up one mystery: I got wind of the little room while being erased. But it stuck in my mind somehow. And now I have dreams about it."

"No."

"What do you mean, *no*?"

"It is the one thing they said could not happen. You could have no recollection of that room."

I grinned. "Shows how much *they* know. I'm wise to their Data Bank, can monkey with their mechs, run their underground maze and even fly this buggy here. And now you tell me I'm not supposed to remember their little white room. Give me a break, lady—the Overseers really loused up on this erasure session. It's a wonder I don't remember my name and ID number. The way I'm going, it'll probably turn up in my mind any second now."

"You are wrong."

"Come on," I said. "I haven't been wrong *yet*. That's why we made it to this crate, isn't it? Let's toss some credit my way, too. The Overseers have enough going for them without you talking their line."

"I am *not* talking their line."

"That's what it sounds like."

"You fail to understand."

"So enlighten me."

"Perhaps your erasure *was* faulty."

"No maybes about it."

"But that is beside the point. There is no way you could remember. All enter the erasure chamber in a state of unconsciousness. And leave the identical way!"

"But I *do* remember."

"Yes. From *somewhere else.*"

"Like where? The city with those long, pretty towers? My dream city?"

"Perhaps."

"Sure. Why not? It's all the same to me. Possibly I saw it on some public tour, right?"

"You did not."

"I didn't, huh?"

"It is quite impossible."

"I like the way you're so sure of things. For a lady who doesn't even know her own name, you show a lot of confidence."

"The others who retained their identities, they told me."

"Nothing like secondhand gossip, is there?"

The girl's eyes blazed at me. "None had heard of the erasure chamber before. They came from many worlds, but of this they were certain. And they were afraid, too. For having seen so much, they feared they might never be allowed to return home. *It is forbidden knowledge.*"

They showed up as five dots high in the western sky. Grew brighter as they moved closer. "Company," I told the girl.

My hand reached out. I turned a knob and the ship went off auto.

Down below was darkness. I didn't waste any effort staring into the dark. I lowered the craft straight down.

The ground rose toward us.

I kept the landing lights off.

The girl peered out the window. "Trees below."

"Thanks."

I leveled off, skirted the treetops, glanced up. The aircraft—whatever they were—were still headed our way. They wouldn't be able to casually spot us—we were down too low. But if they were a search party, they'd have hardware aboard that could do the job. I couldn't outrun them, either—not in a hovercraft, but I could pour on the steam and gain a few minutes. Possibly a few minutes was all I needed.

I told the girl, "Look through your printouts. There should be a close-up of this area." I glanced down at the control panel, gave her our co-ords. The girl got busy with the maps.

I gave ground level the once-over again. All I could see were tops of trees.

The girl said, "What are we seeking?"

"Someplace to hide."

"I have the proper map. The forest below stretches for many links."

"Great."

"There is an old mining site here."

"Where's here?"

"Forty links west."

"Forget it. We need cover now, not later."

I looked up again at our visitors. They would have reached us long ago if they'd been making a beeline in our direction. But they were flying toward us at an angle. I wondered if I ought to just ignore them and go about my business.

As I watched, one of the bright circles of light detached itself from the others, began moving toward us.

"Let me see that map," I said.

The printout passed from the girl's hand to mine. I gave it a long, hard look. A stream wound its way through the trees five links from us, cut a slim line through the forest. There was nothing else. I made for it.

The bright circle behind us was taking up more of the sky now.

Closing my eyes for an instant, I rummaged through my mind, went over what I knew about the hovercraft.

A break suddenly occurred in the mass of treetops. The dark ribbon below was the stream.

I aimed our ship toward it.

The girl's eyes widened as the water came up to meet us.
he didn't say a word as the craft splashed into the stream.

We sank straight down.

Murky darkness overhead, on all sides of us.

I turned to my companion. "As good a place as any. Let's
ope we don't spring a leak."

She tried a half-smile on her face. "I had no idea," she
aid, "we could do such a thing."

"Me, neither—till I thought about it."

"It too was hidden in your mind?"

"I'm a master when it comes to hovercraft. Go on, ask me
nything about them. I can probably make a living off
overcraft, from now on."

"We merely wait?"

"Yeah. Sit tight. We got enough oxygen in here to last
ossibly an hour. The craft is airtight, watertight. As long as
e keep the power off they won't be able to spot us down
ere. Our pals upstairs aren't going to hang around forever.
hey might not even have noticed us. Or if they did, made
othing of it. They won't be looking for us in a hovercraft,
nyway; not till morning, at the earliest."

"Then why are we hiding here?"

"Just in case."

"In case *what?*"

I grinned at her. "In case I'm wrong."

We were silent for a moment. The girl seemed lost in
hought. I looked out at the water around us. A weed
oated by.

The girl was speaking to me. "Why must we go to this
ther prison?"

"I thought you knew. To get a pilot."

"But the risk is *great.*"

"Sure. Everything we do is risky. It's unavoidable."

"But why can't *you* pilot a spaceship?"

"Simple. I don't know how."

"You didn't know how to drive a hovercraft. But it came
o you."

"Not everything comes to me."

"Perhaps pressure brings it out?"

"I've thought of that. I just don't know. Sometimes it
works, sometimes it doesn't. Thing is, a spaceship's no place

83

for on-the-job training. I don't even know how to get one off the ground, let alone navigate. If we louse up at the spaceport, we're not likely to get a second chance."

"Then we continue?"

"Yeah. It's not just our best out, it's our only one."

— CHAPTER —
Fourteen

Block turned over on his side. The room was dim. Faint light spilled through the windows, splashed long shadows against the walls. Sounds of traffic came from outside mixed with the voices of pedestrians. It was eleven-thirty at night, but Soho was just coming alive.

Nora moved against him.

"So *now?*" she said.

"Fine," he said, "now."

"If you fall asleep in the middle, I'll poke you in the ribs."

"Sounds like fun."

"It won't be."

"Don't worry, I'll finish."

"To finish, you've got to begin."

"Right. First off, I told Cohen. That's what you wanted. Well, you've got it. Congratulations."

"What I *really* wanted, honey, was for Cohen to pull you off this story."

"Fat chance. Although he almost did."

"What stopped him?"

"My enthusiasm, I suppose."

"You convinced him it was Nash?"

"I convinced me too. There's more. Nash was a loan-shark, which means protection, mob connections."

"When, recently?"

"Uh-uh. Mid-sixties. Gives him time to rise in the organization, step on enough toes and get rubbed out."

"Or he could have left the rackets altogether."

"Then that's that, no problems, minor story."

"But it still sounds dangerous, sweetie."

"Listen. I'm safer now than I was this morning."

"You can't con me, I know you too well."

"Fine, the facts: this morning I was the only guy working this angle, right? No one else even *knew* about it."

"Except me."

"*Our* secret. No one at the paper, at least. So get rid of me and there goes the story. Now, that's out."

"Because of Ben Cohen."

"Yes, and not just him. I'm getting some help on this, asked for it. And if there *is* a story, I get to break it. Cohen's words. By myself, I could be running around for weeks. This should hurry things along. And it takes the heat off me, too. Sullivan is poking into Nick Siscoe; he may have bankrolled Marty, we'll see. Our boy Max Lewis has been covering organized crime for a couple of decades. He'll ask around, find out which outfit ran the Brooklyn show in the sixties, maybe tie Nash to them. Sandy Gruson will work the credit angle, do a computer check on Marty, see what comes up. And someone'll go through police files, even pester the feds. By the time we're done, we'll have a pretty good notion of what Nash was doing all these years. I hope."

"All this activity makes things *safer?*"

"Sure. Damn mob isn't going to knock off half the paper, is it? Wouldn't do any good anyway. Once the *Register*'s on a story, the secret is out, it becomes public property."

"How about just putting you in the hospital—as an example, sort of?"

"Let them try."

"Think they wouldn't dare?"

"Oh, they'd dare, all right."

"So?"

"So we keep our eyes open, back to the wall and finger on the trigger."

"Reporters carry guns?"

"Only figuratively. The power of the press protects us."

"You wish."

"It better. Hospitals depress me."

They were both silent. Outside on West Broadway an argument of some sort had broken out. Block could hear

85

yelling, voices raised in anger. He didn't bother getting up to see what it was all about. Fracases were a dime a dozen. Manhattan Island was a bubbling pot that periodically boiled over. About every five minutes, according to the police blotter. As long as it happened out there and to someone else, he didn't mind too much. In the morning he'd get to see the damage, view the latest stiffs in the morgue, chat with Rollings or whatever cop was handling the case, seek out the victim's friends, relatives and distant acquaintances, try to get a usable quote. And often even have a nice chat with the perpetrator as he sat handcuffed in the station house. Block got to meet a lot of people, most of whom he didn't like. All part of the job, he knew, and probably a darn sight better than sitting home and reviewing someone else's books or dogging a congressman's footsteps, hanging on his every insipid word. Only sometimes it didn't feel that way.

"Ross."

"Uh-huh."

"What if you get your story?"

"A number of things, if I'm lucky. Cohen goes upstairs, asks old man Ashley to give me a column."

"And if Ashley disagrees?"

"Why should he? Ashley doesn't give a damn as long as the *Register* turns a buck."

"You want to stay with the paper?"

"Think I'm nuts? A column would just be a way to get noticed. I could end up with a syndicate, or another paper, maybe; a better one."

"Sounds nice, honey."

"You're telling me? But if things didn't break my way, if the column went by the boards, I might still get assigned to a better-class story; that would count for something, too. It all depends how far I can take this Nash thing, how much mileage I can get out of it."

"I'm sorry if I sounded so negative before."

"It's okay."

"I know how much this means to you, Ross. But it *is* a bit scary."

"It's a lot scary. Look what some people did to poor Nash. Who probably—unlike old innocent me—had it coming. Still, it should work out fine, now."

"What's next on your agenda?"

"Think I'll check out Charles Hastings' firm."

"Why, honey?"

"Couple of reasons. Did some snooping in the phonebook today. Our pal Nash was a landlord for a while, owned a building. I got his office address off an old rent receipt. I looked up Hastings just for kicks. Guess what? Same address. Then I called downtown—records—had them do a check on Nick Siscoe. At the time of his death, Siscoe had worked for McCoy Imports. That's Hastings' outfit. So what I do first is pay McCoy Imports a call."

"And then what?"

"Follow my nose. But only till six."

"What happens at six?"

"We have dinner and take in a show."

"Best offer I've had in two hours."

"Sure. Think I'm a workhorse?"

"Be careful, Ross."

"Don't worry, sweetie, I'm no hero."

— CHAPTER —

Fifteen

Pitch dark.

I looked behind me. I could hardly see the top of the hovercraft. The rest of it was buried in shrubbery. The ship was all but invisible, would stay that way for the next five hours, till daybreak. After that, it was anyone's guess.

We'd come in over the wall, which divided the penal zone from the rest of Sector Fourteen. Lots of zones in the sector. And I'd picked the toughest nut to crack, the one all the maties wanted out of. It made me wonder if the girl's suggestion that I try something—anything—else didn't have some logic to it after all.

We'd gone about fifty paces when I called a halt.

We stood in the dark, listened to the silence. I tried to spot a landmark, something that might tell us which way to head; there wasn't any.

"We are lost?" the girl whispered.

"Just misplaced," I said. "Still got the map?"

The girl handed me the printout. Shielding the glower, I took a look.

We'd come down near the wall's northwest corner. My first target was a power station some quarter link away. There were a couple of buildings—staff dormitories, mostly—between it and us. I decided to skirt them, go through a wooded area instead. Our jaunt would take a while longer, but we'd make up in safety what we lost in time.

That's what I thought, anyway.

I was wrong.

The first sentry we met had his back to us. I hunted around, found a thick branch, tiptoed behind him and whacked him over the noodle. I tied the sentry's hands and feet and gagged him with strips torn from his own uniform; I left him lying on the ground and trotted off with his gun, a long-nosed blaster. I hadn't been glad to see him, but the blaster made it better, if not wonderful.

"What was he doing there?" the girl asked. I told her I didn't know. The map had shown nothing much worth guarding in this area.

I was peering in the darkness, scouting the territory ahead, when we ran across two more sentries.

They were standing by a wire fence. Neither was facing our way. That was a bit of luck. I motioned for the girl to step back into the woods. I took her hand. We got out of there.

We headed right, till the fence gave out, then continued south in our original direction.

"Beats a rumpus, doesn't it? Only we've lost two much time," I complained, "taking this detour."

"We have a schedule?"

"I'm not sure how long it'll take to fix things at the power station."

"Power station?"

"Yeah. That's our first stop."

"Not the prison?"

"Can't. Got to set the stage first."

"You wish to put out the lights?"

"Something like that."

"There is more?"

"Lots."

The alloy-plus-domed structure was where the printout put it.

The sentry was the big surprise.

At my old work zone the few guards hanging around were just for show. But then, all the maties were Blanks; it made a difference, one I hadn't bothered to consider.

"You could shoot him," the girl said. "From here."

I looked down at my blaster. "That's all we need. These things make noise. We'd have the whole camp down on our heads in no time."

The girl thought it over. "I could go speak to him."

"Yeah, he'd probably like that. But what's in it for us?"

"It would distract him."

"Darn right it would."

"And you could creep up behind him."

I let her idea wiggle through my brain. "Not half bad," I said, "but we can do it even better."

"Better?" The girl sounded puzzled.

"Always room for improvement. Take that blouse you've got on—what if you unbuttoned it maybe? And mussed your hair, got most of it over your face, so if our pal out there took a gander at your mug shot, he still won't make you so fast."

"And what is he to think of my approaching him in this way?"

"Anything he wants. Who cares, as long as you catch his attention?"

"I will certainly do that."

"Look," I said, "this is no time to stand on principle. We've got to get rid of that guard. And with the least possible ruckus."

The girl hesitated, began unbuttoning her blouse. "I do this unwillingly," she said.

"Of course you do. And I appreciate it. You might stagger a bit, too, when you get out there. As though you were drunk or dazed."

"He will think I was raped."

"Yeah. If he has that turn of mind. I'm going to make m
way around to the south side of the station so I'll be behind
him when you step out of the woods. When you see me star
for him, you might fall down or something. Just to keep him
interested."

"I could always disrobe," the girl said icily.

"That's a thought, too, but possibly too obvious. Give
me a while to get in place. Got all that?"

"I am not feebleminded."

The girl was done with her preparations. I looked her ove
and admired the results. I decided not to tell her; she wa
getting touchy.

I waved once, trotted off into the darkness.

She came weaving and bobbing out of the woods. Blond
hair flew over her face, around her neck and shoulders. He
blouse was half off her left shoulder, open to the navel.

For an instant I all but forgot my own job, I was so bus
taking in the sights.

I wasn't the only one.

The guard had his back to me. I couldn't see his face. Bu
I had a pretty good idea it was showing some amazement.

Then the girl fell down.

She didn't just fall. She lifted her arms, seemed to clutch
at the air. Her neck twisted sideways. One leg was hal
raised. Her whole body seemed to shudder. She stiffened
And plopped over on the ground.

I almost applauded.

The guard yelled something, started forward.

I ran after him on the balls of my feet. There could have
been five of me running and the guard wouldn't've paid u
any mind.

I swung the blaster, laid its long barrel neatly behind hi
right ear.

He crumpled without a sound.

The girl was getting to her feet; I was stooped over
reaching for the sentry's blaster when the door to the power
station opened.

The sound warned me.

I straightened and turned in one movement.

There were two of them. The guard's yell must have

roused them. Neither was in uniform, nor carried weapons. Techs, probably. That was good. A blaster going off would've ruined my play, not to mention *me*. Both were big. That was bad. This gladiator business was okay as long as I didn't have to put it to the test too often. I was in no shape to take on all comers.

I didn't let this thought stand in my way.

I hurled myself at the pair.

Astonishment was on both their faces. That gave me hope.

I swung my blaster.

The shorter of the two went down.

Something exploded against my jaw. I was sitting on the ground looking up at a large very angry man. His fists were clenched. He took a step in my direction. My eyes searched for the blaster. It was lying nearby—just out of reach. The man raised his foot and kicked at me. A mistake. My hands moved, caught his foot and twisted.

The man joined me on the ground.

I didn't give him a chance to poke me again. I pounded his face. I lost count how many times. He stopped squirming, went limp. I looked around.

The other one was getting to his feet.

The girl scooped up my blaster, smashed it against his head. He went down again. This time he stayed down.

She gave me her arm. I got to my feet, reluctantly. I wanted to lie there with the two techs and take a rest. I had it coming.

"Still think I'm a gladiator?" I asked.

"You are merely out of practice." She was busy buttoning her blouse.

I dragged both of my victims through the open door of the power station. At least now I wouldn't have to break into the place and risk setting off a siren; my two pals had saved me the trouble.

I trussed them up with their belts and strips from their shirts. The job didn't take long; I'd been getting plenty of practice lately.

The girl and I made our way inside the station. The walls were smooth plasto-deck, the floors hard alloy. Pale light shone from elongated glowers. We entered a wood-paneled, carpeted office, then another.

"Where are we going?" the girl asked.

"We give this place a look-see first, make sure we aren't disturbed during the next hour or so; then we get busy in their control center."

"Which is where?"

"Somewhere around here. Or they wouldn't've built the station, right? We can't miss."

We didn't. We hit control some ten minutes later. No one about; the center had been programmed to mostly run itself. I gave the large hardware-decked room a quick going-over and moved on. Another ten minutes finished our tour. We had the place to ourselves. That's all I wanted to know. We went back to control. Time to get to work.

— CHAPTER —
Sixteen

Block lay on the lumpy cot.

Someone at the far end of the loft screamed, had been doing so on and off for the last quarter hour. Block paid no attention. The stink of unwashed bodies hung in the air like thick gray fog, mixed with the odor of cheap pine-scented disinfectant. Sleeping men shifted restlessly across the aisle to the right and left of him. The long, narrow loft was alive with murmurs, a tired chorus of groans, broken words, and phrases.

Pale light from a pair of streetlamps shone through the grimy windows, made a crosshatch of shadows on peeling walls and ceiling. Traffic noises came from the street below.

He sighed, stared at the ceiling. It floated above him like a living thing, spinning and shaking. *Drunk*. He was drunk. But obviously not drunk enough—he still couldn't sleep.

The glow of red neon lights caught the edge of the cracked windowpane. He knew without looking what they spelled out: Transients' Hotel. Flophouse would've been more like it. At that he was lucky—better off here than in the gutter, or at the Men's Shelter where they dumped you in their Big Room and you sat up all night on a hard plastic chair with a bunch of jabbering loonies for company. Yeah, for a bum he was lucky, all right. But for anyone else, he'd reached the end of the line.

He must have dozed; he couldn't be sure. The night seemed darker, deeper, the light more subdued. Even the street sounds were muffled and distant as if someone had wrapped him in a thick blanket. He began to raise his wrist, bring the watch to his eyes, when he remembered there was no watch. His hand sank back against the bed, lay there like a dead thing.

He glanced at the ceiling. It was just a ceiling now, had stopped twisting like a snake. Not so good. He was sobering up.

Block closed his eyes, tried desperately to drift back to sleep. The flickers would be gone then; he'd be at peace. The cot seemed as soft as a concrete slab. His clothes bunched up under him, making a series of small hills and valleys beneath his body. He'd bedded down fully dressed right to his shoes. Stripping in this joint would've only been an invitation for the fleas and bedbugs to send for their relatives. Besides, Block knew none of his clothing would have been likely to be around come morning. His bunk-mates left something to be desired in the way of character; in fact, he wasn't doing so hot in that department himself, was he?

Spitefully, sleep wouldn't come.

Block tossed and turned, waiting for the night to end, no idea how long that might take. In the morning he'd make a touch, start the booze flowing again; he'd be all right then. His hands had begun to shake, and he wondered if he could hold out that long.

Down the far-right side of the loft, below the lit exit sign, he saw the door slowly sliding open. He almost grinned. Anyone creeping around after hours in this dump was probably up to no good. But so what? All he wanted was to be let alone.

Stray light reached through the windows, cut small crooked patches out of the darkness.

Block lay, his head to one side, eyes open, idly peering toward the door.

Someone stood in the doorway, lost in the shadows. Block couldn't make out the face or figure. He didn't care; he had lots of time to satisfy what little curiosity he had left.

Presently, a shape detached itself from the blackness— one wearing hat and coat—and began moving stealthily from bunk to bunk. Block wasn't surprised. The guy was hunting for a wallet, a piece of loose change. Some bum off the street probably who'd slipped by the downstairs clerk. He'd need more than luck to come up with two bits from this crew, Block thought; he'd need a minor miracle.

Block considered letting out a holler, and rejected the notion: it would take too much effort. The man, he saw, was moving fast, had already covered a fourth of the loft.

And somehow that wasn't right.

He was in too much of a hurry, hadn't even stopped to frisk the marks; he paused only an instant over each bunk. It didn't make sense. What did he want?

The man straightened up, stepped into the aisle where darkness gave way to dim light. Block saw his face.

It was a long, narrow face, the lips thin, the nose flat. He wasn't wearing a slick black suit this time, but Block knew who this was just the same. *The man from the flickers!*

The shock caught him like a giant fist in the guts; he had trouble breathing. He felt his arms and legs turning to soft, pliant jelly.

Just six beds from the fire door which led down the back staircase and out. He could jump up and dive through that door.

Only he'd never make it.

Block wondered if he could slip off the cot, crawl under it and hide. Not bad, but a bit late. The flicker man was only a couple of beds away.

His hands were empty. No weapon in sight. The gun or knife would be in his pocket; he'd have to reach for it, and that, Block knew, would be his one chance to make a move.

Move?

Where? In what direction?

Block narrowed his eyes to mere slits, lay very still. The flicker man was bending over him, peering down. Block glimpsed a gloved hand sliding toward an overcoat pocket.

Block stopped thinking.

He brought his knees up to his chest in one swift motion. The flicker man, half stooped, tried to straighten, step sideways at the same time.

Block kicked out.

The flicker man went over backward onto the next cot. Block took off in the opposite direction, landed on the floor.

He was on his feet without knowing how he'd gotten there. His fingers groped for the edge of the cot. He flung cot, mattress and blanket at the tall figure struggling to rise.

He ran for the stairs.

His legs got tangled and he almost went down. A voice was whimpering somewhere—a voice that sounded suspiciously like his own. Block jerked open the door, all but fell through. He didn't look back, headed down the dark staircase, taking two and three stairs at a time. The jolts racked his body, buckled his knees with each step, his lungs were on fire, and he wanted to scream, but couldn't.

Behind him, the fire door banged open.

Block doubled over, dived down the few remaining steps, crashed to the floor.

He'd come to rest against the outside street door.

He clawed at it with shaking hands, pushed and shoved. No dice; it wouldn't budge. Reaching up in the darkness, his fingers frantically groped for the latch.

Something hard smacked into the door's wooden frame above him. *The flicker man had a gun and silencer!*

Block tore at the latch with all his strength. It popped open. He twisted the knob, put his shoulder against the door and rolled out onto the street.

A bullet sent pavement chips flying near his face. He drew a sobbing breath, crawled sideways out of the line of fire.

Streetlamps lit the block. Darkness wouldn't hide him anymore. He glanced wildly to his right and left. He was alone—not even a passing car. He stared at the door. No way to lock it from the outside.

Block opened his mouth, bawled, "He's in there, he's got a gun; watch out!"

He lurched to his feet, stumbled up the block. He'd been talking to himself, but the flicker man on the staircase couldn't know that; maybe it would give him an instant's pause.

He rounded the corner, going full tilt, hit a side street of old ramshackle tenements. It was dark here, but not dark enough, and just as deserted.

He ran up to the nearest house, flung open the door. He was in a four-foot alcove; the inner door was locked tight.

Too late to go back on the street. And odds had it this would be the first place the flicker man would look; any house farther down would've been better.

Block searched in his pants pockets, came up with a crumpled pack of matches; shakily he lit one. A row of buzzers glittered in the light. He had nothing to lose. He pressed one at random, then another. Silence. He flattened his palm against them all and pressed down hard.

A second later Block got his answer, more than one.

He shoved open the door, stepped through, heard it click shut behind him. Total darkness. Somewhere upstairs a man's voice called, "Yeah?" The voice didn't sound friendly.

Block kept his mouth shut. He was more likely to get thrown back into the street than given help. He was a mess. Who would believe a disheveled bum was being chased by a murderous gunman? He hardly believed it himself.

Standing in the darkness, Block heard the outside door squeak open.

Without thinking, he moved down the hallway. He was going to be sick. He tried not to make any noise, to keep from whimpering. Up front he heard the sound of someone being buzzed in.

His legs turned to rubber under him. He felt as if he'd been running uphill for long, endless miles.

The inner door creaked open just as Block touched—what had to be—the rear wall. A back exit couldn't be far away. Quietly he ran his trembling fingers across the wall.

"Who the hell is it?" an angry voice called from upstairs.

Block's hand brushed a doorframe, found a knob, turned it gently. Nothing doing.

"You better beat it," the voice yelled down, "before I call the cops. You hear?"

He found the bolt, lifted it, eased open the door, praying that the tenant's voice had covered his movements, stepped into a backyard.

He hobbled for the fence at the end of the yard — a five-footer made of wood. It took him two tries to get over.

Block huddled on the ground, too spent to move. He was just as likely to crash into a trash can as make a clean getaway if he took to his feet; he could hardly walk, let alone run.

Block managed to get his eye next to a crack in the fence, peer through. At first, there was only darkness, then he began to distinguish shapes: the yard, the tenement house, the door through which he'd come. It was open. The figure of a man in hat and coat was barely visible in the doorway. Block tried not to move, not to breathe. Sweat rolled down his forehead, streamed into his eyes. He blinked, looked again. The doorway was empty, the man gone.

— CHAPTER —

Seventeen

I took a last squint at the power station.

The girl's hand slipped into mine. We ran for it.

A gravel road gave way to a concrete walk. Trees and shrubbery became sparse. Buildings of all shapes and sizes started filling the landscape: square, round, domed and something that looked as though it had warts on it. We kept going. More structures appeared as we got closer to zone center. We left the lighted walk, took to shadows. A good-sized town had sprung up around us in the twenty-five minutes we'd been jogging. No lights shone through the streets. The whole zone here, according to our map, was admin, given over to offices, warehouses, processing depots for the prison complex.

The girl squeezed my hand, asked, "We are on schedule?" She was breathless from our pace. Or possibly excitement. I was feeling it too.

We could see the prison ahead. Not a pleasant sight. It

looked like a large black slab, a hollowed-out tombstone.

"Look at that—" I began.

The sound came from behind us, a ground car of some sort. I cut short my speech. The girl and I ran for cover.

Crouching in a narrow alley between two small alloy buildings, we watched the car rumble by. It was an open-topped six-wheeler. Four warders sat inside. Two of them were men. The others were something else. A floodlight on the hood lit the darkness. The car slid around a corner, was gone. I let out my breath.

The girl whispered, "For us?"

I thought it over. "Doubtful. The nightwatch, possibly. If it were us—something big—there'd be more commotion. The streets'd be crawling with 'em."

"They will be soon enough."

"Yeah, But they'll have other things on their minds."

We left our hideout, continued on our way. The girl clutched my arm. Between breaths she asked, "We truly have a chance now, do we not?"

"You bet," I told her.

"And it has never, never been done!"

"So they say. You believe them?"

"Yes."

"Very trusting. But that's all before *we* came along, isn't it?" I grinned at her and myself in the darkness. I'd said it. But did I really believe it?

The prison up close looked more like a fortress than a tombstone. High stone walls circled the main building. The courtyard inside was alloy, offered no place to hide or take cover. The main building—where the maties were kept—was windowless. Searchlights poked into the darkness on all sides of the wall.

The girl and I huddled in back of a tin storage shed. No sounds. The stillness was starting to get on my nerves, a constant reminder of where we were. And what we were up against. At least we'd hear the patrol if it came here again.

I glanced down at the ground. I wouldn't have minded a bit of shut-eye. And possibly a four-course dinner while I was at it. My breakout had jumped the gun, caught me unprepared. I'd neglected to bring along a small something to keep the body in working order, an oversight. I was regretting more with the passing of each hour.

"How're you doing?" I asked the girl.

"Fine." She didn't sound sincere.

I could hardly see her face in the gloom.

"Hungry?" I asked.

A toss of her long blond hair was the only answer I got. I took that for a yes.

"Can you hang on?"

"Of course. And if I had said no?"

"I'd worry."

"You are not worried now?"

"I'd worry more."

"I owe you so much—" she began.

"It's the other way around," I told her. "Without you I'd still be back at the Data Bank."

"I do not believe it."

"Take my word. Their computer's a mystery to me. You've earned the breakout prize, and then some."

The girl sighed, put a hand on my arm. Her voice was low. "Should we *not* succeed, I wish—"

"Forget that."

"Please. You must know. I will always remember what you have done—"

I almost laughed. "*Always.* In our case that won't be too long, will it? Not with the erasure chamber all ready and waiting. Nice thought, anyway."

We were quiet.

The girl said, "What if they are right?"

"Right?"

"The Overseers."

"Right about *what?*"

"Us."

"Being public enemies?"

"Yes."

"Nuts."

"No, really."

"That's their lookout."

"But sometimes I wonder if—"

"If you're guilty."

Her fingers tightened on my arm. "The thought is always with me. Always."

"Only natural. It's part of the treatment. Helps keep the

maties in line. Makes 'em think they deserve all this."

"But do they not know—?"

"Some of them; they know everything, except why they're here. That part's been erased."

Her hand had grown cold in mine.

"You are certain?" she whispered.

"Yeah."

"It is peculiar that you should know this."

I grinned. "Just part of my wisdom."

"You think you were poorly erased."

"That's what I think."

"But it is *what* you know that is so strange."

I shook my head. "Could be. But it's saving our necks, isn't it?"

"That is not the point. Have you considered—" She broke off.

"Go on," I said.

She took a deep breath. "That you were one of them once?"

"Them?"

"The Overseers."

The first blast turned the sky a brilliant white. It came from the northeast, about three links away. The ground rocked under our feet. A second blast battered our eardrums. The third shook the walls of the storage shed, all but knocked me to my knees. I put my arm around the girl, tried to steady us both.

The night wasn't black anymore.

Red flame reared skyward—a solid sheet of link-wide flame.

Sirens had begun to blare, mixed with the sounds of smaller explosions.

The night had come alive.

My face wore a lopsided grin. I wasn't tired or hungry anymore.

I turned to the girl and laughed. "How about that?"

Again the night seemed to split in two. This time from the northwest. Flame bubbled up from the ground, yellow flame with streaks of orange in it.

"Fuel depot." I grinned. "That should give 'em something to remember us by, huh?"

The girl eyed the flaming chaos in the distance. We could feel the heat now, smell the fumes.

More sirens joined the clamor—along with shouting voices, racing engines as cars took to the roadways. The sounds came from up ahead. But where we were, near the prison, there was only darkness.

I heard myself laugh again, a high-pitched crazy sound.

The girl's voice was in my ear. "You are enjoying this too much."

"Yeah. Don't I know it."

I'd used the printouts, picked the targets. The girl had put the computer on override, programmed a triple dose of voltage. Overload had done the rest. Electric power had come pouring through conduits, melting circuits, bursting through walls, floors, ceilings. I laughed again as the power station—having finished its job—turned on itself, went up in a shattering roar!

Blue-red flame scorched the sky.

Throughout the entire zone lights snapped off.

"Okay," I told her, "let's move."

— CHAPTER —

Eighteen

Block hurried along the street. Faint light probed the sky; it would be daylight in another hour. The sidewalk seemed pitted and mined with potholes. He had trouble keeping his legs under him. His hands kept twitching.

The flicker man.

The flicker man.

The flicker man had found him!

How?

Better not think about it. Keep walking. Think about something else. Anything. Anything at all.

Gray streets. Stores still locked. A faded sign over one

read Used Clothes, another Bowery Lumber Company. A light burned in the window of the corner gas station; it was the only spot open for business. Across the street, the Grand Hotel—a fleabag he'd often slept in—was dark, except for one window.

The odor of rotting garbage came to him from trash cans, alleyways. The street kept drifting in and out of focus. He half expected the flicker man to come waltzing out of some doorway.

The flicker man.

The flicker man.

Block suddenly found he couldn't walk. His head was whirling and the street seemed to tip like a raft shooting the rapids.

The flickers came.

He had the gun in his hand. Again.

The crowd was screaming. As it always did.

He felt his finger tighten on the trigger. And knew he was smiling.

The man backed up, his hand half raised as if to fend off the shot.

Sound seemed to fill the room as he squeezed the trigger.

The man hurtled against the wall; blood spurted from his mouth. He crumpled to the floor.

The tall, thin guy with the long face and flat nose stepped out of the crowd. He wore a narrow black suit, was reaching for his gun.

The flickers went on and off, on and off like a shorted neon sign.

The flat-nosed guy slowly aimed his gun.

Block knew he was moving backward; his own gun felt heavy in his hand.

Again, the sound of a blast seemed to rock the walls.

Sound and sight mixed together. Flickered. And died.

Block lay face down on the pavement.

He got to his hands and knees, began very slowly, crawling toward a car parked at the curb. He rested by the front tire, then hoisted himself up, using tire and hood.

It took a while before he started walking again. His feet felt as if they'd been encased in granite. It was all he could do to lift one after another.

The flicker man had stepped out of the flickers and had come after him.

The flicker man was going to even the score. And there was nothing he could do about it, not even go to the cops; least of all go to the cops.

Because he was guilty.

The Big Room at the men's shelter was almost empty. The rows of worn plastic chairs seemed naked without their allotment of bums. At night Block knew the place would be packed solid. But now there was only the lingering stench of unwashed bodies, three deadbeats sacked out in their chairs, and old Knobby pushing his broom over by the window.

"Hiya, Mr. Block."

Only Knobby ever called him mister anymore. If the floor sweep had a last name, Block didn't know it. The little man had been good for a handout once before. Block was desperate now, afraid to hang around on the streets trying to panhandle. Not with the flicker man gunning for him.

"Whaddya say, Knobby?"

"Another day, another dollar, eh, Mr. Block?" He was bald, skinny, somewhere in his sixties, dressed in a white T-shirt and baggy pants.

Block ran a hand through his hair, reached a decision. "Listen, I'm gonna tell you somethin'."

"Always ready to lend an ear, Mr. Block. Part of the job."

"This is gonna sound nutty—"

"Never fear, Mr. Block. I've seen and heard them all."

"Yeah, sure. Listen. There was this guy, see? And he tried to shoot me."

"Shoot you?" Knobby smiled.

"Yeah. I was sleeping in this fleabag and this guy pops up—"

"A fellow guest?"

"Uh-uh. He came through the door. It was late at night; I kept waking up—"

"And you two had a row?"

"What row? He tried to shoot me."

Knobby shook his head. "Must have been a reason, Mr. Block. That's only common sense."

"Yeah. No. He tried once before."

"You knew him, then?"

"Shit! Don't know him from Adam."

"Maybe you imagined the whole thing, Mr. Block?"

"Jesus, this was real! He tried to shoot me."

"*But why, Mr. Block?*"

Block thought it over, decided against spilling his guts; they'd make Knobby be a witness against him. "Beats me," he said weakly.

Knobby grinned. "You're pulling my leg."

"Uh-uh. So help me. This guy wants to kill me. He's come looking for me."

"You're excited, Mr. Block. No one's come looking for you—" Knobby broke off.

"What is it?"

"Hold on a minute, Mr. Block, someone *has* been asking about you."

"What do you mean? Who?"

"Didn't say. A man. About three days ago."

"Tall guy? Thin lips? Flat nose? Kind of skinny?"

"Not really, Mr. Block. This one was tall, all right, but pudgy. Had red hair and a big chin. Asked for you by name, he did, wanted to know where you were."

"What did you tell him?"

"Nothing. You could have been anywhere."

"Thanks, Knobby."

"Don't mention it, Mr. Block. Glad to oblige."

"Yeah, listen, I gotta get outta here. They're lookin' for me, don't you see?"

"You in some kind of trouble, Mr. Block?"

Block nodded. "Yeah, I'm in a jam. Can you help me out, Knobby? I'm busted, flat broke. And I gotta duck."

Knobby stuffed a bony hand in his pocket, brought out some loose change. "It's all I can spare, Mr. Block."

"Thanks, Knobby, thanks."

"Think nothing of it, Mr. Block. Your collateral covers this too."

"Yeah, sure." Block was already headed for the door. "Gotta go."

"You take care, Mr. Block."

"Jesus."

Block trotted down the street. His hands kept twitching. They were after him, all right; the flicker man needed more blood. He looked around wildly. Only the usual assortment of bums, either sprawled on the sidewalk or shuffling off toward nowhere.

Just like him.

Block tried very hard to think; it was important now. Sure, he'd had a job once, only he wasn't quite certain what it was. He saw himself a jaunty, well-dressed figure, striding down a tree-lined avenue.

Which one?

He didn't know.

There were men and women in his life, but their faces were indistinct.

"Too lushed-up," Block murmured to himself. He hadn't realized he was this far gone. Or had he?

Block tried again:

He was seated at a large desk. The window was open and the room was filled with sunlight. Was he writing something? He could hear footsteps on the other side of the door. . . .

Block looked around. For a moment he didn't know where he was.

Cooper Union — a large, ancient red stone building — was to his right, a parking lot on the left. A street sign said Astor Place.

Jesus, Block thought, his feet had carried him right past skid row. Nothing for him out here. No friends. No family. No job. He had to turn back.

But he couldn't turn back.

No place left to hide on the Bowery; he'd be a sitting duck. Only a matter of time before they ran him down again, squashed him like a bug.

Lots of places a guy could land a drink, hustle some change; what did he need the Bowery for? Not winter yet. A doorway was as good a place as any to bed down. *And out there they'd never find him!*

He crossed the street, started hiking again. He felt better. He'd walk till his feet gave out. Somewhere he'd find a hangout where they'd leave him alone.

For an instant Block saw himself again in clean clothes, hair combed, face shaven. It almost stopped him cold. Something he had to find out, a question he wanted answered. What was it? Block shrugged, kept walking. It couldn't have been very important. Nothing was important anymore.

Nineteen

We got to the wall.

Behind us bright flame lit the night like a giant's idea of a bonfire.

No bells clamored, no sirens wailed — the blowup of the power station had pulled their plug. Instead voices screamed and bellowed in the darkness.

I wondered if turmoil had begun to boil over in the prison yet. The largest doors and gates, all run electronically, would be useless now. The guards would have their hands full trying to secure them. The cell doors themselves were held in place by bolts. It was anyone's guess how long it'd take the maties to figure a way out; I was betting on not too long.

The gate to the outside fence swung open to my touch.

The courtyard was still empty.

All the hubbub was coming from outside. The prison itself was a haven of peace — at least where we were.

I used the glower, looked over a printout. The man we wanted, a space pilot called De-Nor, was in cell block six. Once the maties got loose we'd never find him.

I told the girl, "Stick by my side. This uniform should help inside."

"I am in matie garb," she whispered.

"You're an orderly assigned to me — if someone asks. They won't, not in the middle of this mess. Just don't get lost."

We moved up to the large double front doors. I stopped short.

"I don't like it," I said. "It's too easy, just walking through their front door. That's about the one place they'd keep an eye on. Let's find a more private spot."

The printout showed more doors. I chose one marked kitchen.

We hiked for what felt like a long time but couldn't have been more than two or three minutes. We met no one, heard nothing.

The door we came to opened noiselessly on a darkened interior. Nothing to it. We stepped inside and were back in prison. Silence. And the vague odors of food mixed with those of cleansers, floor wash, dish powder. I flicked on the glower: plasto-deck floors, large tables, stoves, sinks, garbage cans.

"I'm depressed already," I told the girl. "Let's get out of here."

We went along a hallway. Our isolation came to an abrupt end. Voices reached us now, a sea of them, rising and falling somewhere inside the building.

"Swell party," I said.

We turned a lot of corners. The voices kept getting louder. Metal stairs took us up to the next landing. I called a halt, consulted the printout again.

Two guards ran by us. They didn't stop to exchange greetings.

A third guard came racing along the corridor.

"Trouble?" I yelled.

"Cell block one's busted open," he shouted over his shoulder. He rounded a bend, was gone.

"Nuts," I said.

"You think we are too late?"

"Could be. Our boy is three flights up. Let's go see."

We trotted along the hallway. The staircase that would take us up was on the other side of a large hall. We were halfway across it when I heard a door slam open, a chorus of shouting voices.

I turned my light on the commotion.

Men in gray prison garb were pouring through a doorway, their faces wild, eyes half crazed, mouths gaping. Their hands weren't empty either. Some held metal pipes. Others hammers, wrenches, drills, even broomsticks.

I didn't waste time taking inventory. I doused my light before this crew got a look at my uniform and took offense, grabbed the girl's arm and made tracks—in the dark—for the other side of the hall. I hit the wall, groped around, found a doorway and went through it.

Behind us the shouts had turned to a roar as more maties filled the hall. I used my light again. A narrow metal staircase led up.

"Last lap," I said.

I stripped off my tie and jacket, dropped them to the floor, opened up the top three buttons of my shirt, rolled up my sleeves. Maybe I wouldn't pass for a matie, but I didn't look like an Overseer either, anymore. I got my badge out, palmed it. If we ran into some guards, I could always flash it, get waved through. Unless someone looked too close. The girl and I hustled up three flights of stairs. No one came after us.

We stepped out on the fourth-level landing.

The voices were loud, insistent. Some yelled, others cursed, a few seemed to be sobbing.

I shone my light along the corridor. It was empty.

The voices came from cells on both sides of the aisle. A long metal bar ran the length of each wall, held the cell doors in place. The bar could be raised or lowered electronically. It had been in lock position when the power went. And stayed there.

The cells stretched off into darkness. De-Nor was in one of them. The printout neglected to say which one.

I gave my glower to the girl, made a megaphone of my hands and bawled, "De-Nor!"

An instant of dead silence. Then voices started calling back. None identified itself as our pilot. All wanted to be let out.

"Which way to De-Nor?" I yelled.

No one told me. Pleas, cries and threats came through the small, square mesh-lined peephole in each door. Not very enlightening.

"Follow me," I told the girl.

I jogged down the length of the corridor yelling the pilot's name. The girl's scampered behind me. My stomach muscles were busy tying themselves into small useless knots. My stomach knew a thing or two. If we didn't find De-Nor soon, we could stop looking. We rounded a corner, then another.

De-Nor!" I called.

If he heard me, he wasn't doing much about it. At least

there were no signs of guards. I wondered how long that situation would last.

It was getting hard to hear anything in the uproar. The jailed men were becoming more frantic. Along with me.

"De-Nor!" I called again, louder.

Still nothing.

It was beginning to look as though I'd made a wrong choice for pilot. There was still our former Prime Minister buried in the prison somewhere. The computer had tagged him as a pilot. But on what level was he kept? And was he still in place?

"*Still in place, my friend,*" a very clear voice said in my mind.

I almost keeled over. I stopped dead in my tracks, looked around to see if the voice wasn't coming from one of the cells.

"What is it?" the girl asked.

"I heard a voice."

All around us maties were screaming; voices were hardly in short supply.

"De-Nor?" she asked.

"I don't know. It was in my head."

The girl squinted at me sharply. I could sympathize. The last thing we needed now was a voice in my head.

It spoke again:

"*De-Nor is dead.*"

My mouth opened of its own accord. I flicked my light across the cells.

Nothing.

"We cannot stay here," the girl said frantically.

I couldn't have put it any better myself.

I made a heroic effort. Moving one foot in front of the other, I launched myself down the aisle. "De-Nor," I bellowed.

"*It is futile,*" the voice in my mind said.

I stopped. Again. As though riveted to the floor.

The girl tugged at my arm. "Please," she said. Her eyes held panic. From her viewpoint I'd gone off my rocker, stranded us in a pitch-black hallway with maties rioting down below and guards massing in the courtyard for a counterattack. With a lunatic as chief tactician, both of us were sunk. Too bad. I shared her viewpoint.

I looked around one more time, playing my light over walls, floor and ceiling.

"*You are wasting time,*" the voice complained.

"Who are you?" I heard myself say.

"*I am Ganz,*" the voice told me.

"Where are you?" I asked.

"*The ninth level.*"

The girl was pulling at my arm again. I ignored her.

"How are you getting through to me?" I asked.

"*I speak directly to your mind, my friend.*"

"That's nice. Can you speak so that both the girl and I hear you?"

"*Not at the same time.*"

"Okay, tell her something, show her you're real." And me too, I might have added.

The voice in my head went away. I looked at the girl. Her eyes widened, her brow wrinkled. She opened and closed her mouth, a movement I was familiar with; I'd done the exact same thing an instant ago.

"Hear it?" I asked.

She nodded dumbly.

"*You are satisfied?*" Ganz asked me.

"*Yeah,*" I thought back. "*What do you want?*"

"*To help you.*"

"*Why?*"

"*So you will help me.*"

That sounded reasonable. That was about all that was reasonable. I had doused the glower in case someone wandered our way. We stood in darkness. Matie voices still jabbered through peepholes. A voice was chatting calmly in my head. I was becoming very nervous.

Ganz said, "*They knew of my ability to enter minds. They blocked my powers by creating a force field around my cell. I was as helpless as the other maties, my friend, until you disrupted the flow. That freed me. Or rather, it freed my mind to roam.*"

"*And you sized up the situation.*"

Ganz chuckled. "*It was not as simple as that. Or I should have reached you sooner. There were many minds to visit before I could draw the proper conclusions, understand the*

*significance of what was occurring. Then I found you and
the girl. I was going to lead you to De-Nor, but I could not
discover his whereabouts. I whispered his name to some of
my fellow maties. The name provoked the thought of his
demise. I then set out to find a substitute, someone who
could pilot your spaceship. When you mentioned your
Prime Minister, I sought him out. You are quite right, my
friend, he is your man. I can take you to him. But you must
free me."*

"You're five levels up?"

"Yes."

"Sit tight," I thought foolishly. As though this Ganz had a
choice.

The girl asked, "What *is* happening?"

I grinned at her in the darkness. "You wouldn't believe
me if I told you."

We headed back for the staircase. Our light attracted
jeers and hoots from the maties inside their cells; some
called out De-Nor's name tauntingly. Our popularity was
hitting rock bottom.

I paused by the staircase. The rod mechanism which freed
the cell doors was there. An emergency jack in the wall let
me work the left one manually. The girl took the right. Both
rods rose slowly toward the ceiling. It took a while, but the
effort was worth it. Maties came swarming out of their cells,
filled the corridor, hundreds of them. I liked that. The more
maties running loose, the tougher it'd be to find us.

I kept my glower off, took hold of the girl's arm. We went
up. I was getting to know this staircase like a long-lost
brother—one I didn't like.

We covered two levels and were starting on the third when
Ganz popped up in my mind again:

"Three guards are coming down toward you."

"Where?" I thought back.

"Two flights away now. They are armed."

"Great," I murmured; to the girl I whispered, "Hold it,
we've got company."

We backtracked to the sixth level, flattened ourselves
against the metal wall. It felt cold against my sweat-soaked
shirt.

I heard their footsteps before I saw them. Then light danced over the stairs. Three figures hurried past, showed us their backs, started down for the level below.

A thought flashed through my head. I moved before I had time to think it over and change my mind. Instinct took charge. I hoped the gladiator part of me hadn't lost his stuff—our future was riding on him.

Four steps brought me within three feet of the guards.

I swung my blaster, connected with the head of the last one. He toppled forward.

I jumped in close, swung again. A second guard fell.

The last guard turned, his blaster half out of its holster. I smashed my fist into his face. He joined his pals on cloud nine.

I stooped down, helped myself to their guns, handed them to the girl.

We continued our climb. The extra hardware was small comfort; but even small was something.

We hit the ninth level.

I threw a thought at Ganz:

"You aboard?"

"Yes."

"I'm letting some maties out."

"That is most thoughtful of you."

"Yeah, isn't it."

I turned to the girl. "We do the number with the rods again."

We got busy.

The sounds of rods cranking up brought the maties to life. Their voices rose to a shout as cell doors banged open.

I put an arm around the girl; we went up half a flight of stairs toward the tenth level, stood and waited. No one came our way. The crush—yelling, cursing and tripping—piled through the doorway, spilled down the stairs. I wondered how the hotfoot I'd given this zone was faring.

"We're between nine and ten," I told Ganz.

"I shall join you shortly."

"How's the zone out there?"

"It burns, my friend. The Overseers and Warders are quite frantic."

"Frantic?"

"You may take my word for it."

"*That's a bit more than even I figured.*"

"*You used the power station to overload the system.*"

I admitted it.

"*You overrode the computer's program, selected your targets and timed the progression of explosions.*"

"That's the long and short of it," I said.

The voice chuckled in my mind. "*Don't you see, the Overseers never expected an attack of such proportions. Who among the maties would have the knowledge to execute such a strategy? I, perhaps. But the force field rendered me harmless.*"

"They kept you bottled up in your cell?"

"*For two years. The Overseers are far from stupid. But in your case, my friend, they erred. It is quite incredible, you know.*"

"*What is?*"

By now the last of the prisoners had plunged down the stairs. I listened for Ganz's footsteps but heard nothing. His cell must have been at the far end of the aisle—a long way to go.

"*Your knowledge,*" Ganz said in my mind, "*of the power station's location, of the various sites you wished destroyed. The Overseers were totally unprepared for such wholesale destruction. The munitions bin alone was more than they had bargained for.*"

"Yeah, I figured that might do it."

"*It spreads, too, my friend. They cannot contain the flames. It consumes half the zone.*"

I turned to the girl. "Ganz says the place is one large torch out there."

"He communicates with you?"

"Yeah."

"Where is he?"

"On his way."

"I am here," a deep mellifluous voice said from the bottom of the stairwell.

I shone my light down.

He was standing by the doorway, his head raised toward us. He looked human enough, considering what he could do. He was possibly six foot two—my height. He had wide shoulders, a large bald head, high cheekbones. His nose was hooked, lips full. His eyes in the glower's glare seemed jet black.

"I have brought a friend," Ganz said, smiling.

He nodded toward the door.

Ganz was no midget, but the man who stepped through the doorway made him seem so. He was at least seven feet tall. He must have weighed over four hundred pounds. None of it looked like fat. His face was craggy, nose lumpy, lips thick. The hands which hung at his sides were as large as most men's heads. He nodded at me, and did something with his face which I took for a smile. I was glad to see it.

"I am Bar," he said in a rumbling basso.

"Bar's presence will simplify matters," Ganz said. "He commands respect."

"He does mine," I admitted. "Where have they stashed our pilot?"

"Prime Minister Lix-el is on the twenty-first level," Ganz said.

"They couldn't have put him in the basement?" I complained.

"You would not have wanted that," Ganz said. "The basement is the execution chamber."

"You're right," I said.

We started up.

Ganz turned to me. "You were quite correct, my friend, to free the maties. The guards are well occupied. We should free more."

The girl asked, "Will any truly manage to escape?"

Ganz shrugged, smiled. "Our own escape is far from certain, my dear."

"He means no," Bar said, "they have no chance. But it will help cover our tracks."

"We were fortunate," Ganz said, "that an orderly freed the first two levels."

"Hundreds of maties," Bar told us.

"It drew most of the guards from their posts," Ganz said. He sounded pleased.

"Can you tell how it is progressing?" the girl asked.

Ganz said, "The maties are handicapped by a lack of weapons."

Bar said, "Are there guards on the next level?"

"No," Ganz said.

"We should open the cell doors."

We did, pausing on each level to crank the jacks. Bar did

114

both sides of the aisle; he did it fast and made it look easy. The maties always headed down. We kept moving up.

"I have communicated, mentally, with Lix-el," Ganz reported.

"And?" I asked.

"There are no telepaths on his world," Ganz said dryly. "He thought himself going quite mad, but I managed to convince him of his sanity. He has decided to join our party."

I asked, "When did all this happen?"

"Just now."

By the time we'd hit the twenty-first level I was ready to call it a day; we had emptied out a third of a prison. Bar worked the jacks again; he didn't seem to mind.

Ganz said, "The flames have been noted in the adjoining zones. They will send help. We must move with speed now."

The maties took to their heels. Our quartet waited patiently—out of harm's way—till the last one had charged down the stairs to do battle with the authorities.

I shone the light down the empty aisle. All the cell doors were open. A small man strode toward us. He had a large head, skimpy hair over a bald dome. His legs were short, his belly stuck out over his belt. He squinted at us, and I lowered the glower. He didn't look much like my idea of a pilot. But I wasn't sure my ideas were up to snuff anymore—I'd been a Blank too long.

Ganz and Bar introduced themselves to the little man.

"I see," he said. He looked at me and the girl. "And you two?"

"Just numbers on someone's card," I said.

"Erased you, did they?"

"Yeah. You really a pilot?"

"Of course not. I'm a politician, young man. But flying is one of my hobbies."

"Think you can handle a spaceship?"

"Certainly. If we can reach the spaceport."

"We'll try," Bar rumbled.

"Get me a spaceship," the Prime Minister said, "and I will fly you out of here."

— CHAPTER —
Twenty

The sun was directly overhead by the time Block reached Third Avenue and Seventy-eighth Street. He'd made the trip in a semi-daze, his legs dragging him along, but his head was somewhere else. He wasn't sure exactly where.

Now he stopped to look around.

There was nothing different about this corner, nothing to catch his attention.

But something had.

Peering around him, he saw a candy store, a fruit and vegetable market, a butcher shop. He must've passed dozens like them on his stroll from the Bowery, but these seemed different.

How?

Block stood stock-still, his head swiveling from right to left. Did he know this place, had he been here before?

He tried to figure out when and where. An image formed in his mind: *He was in a room, seated at a desk; he seemed to be writing something.*

What room?

Shit. Who gave a damn? He shrugged, started to move on, stopped; he couldn't shake the feeling.

He crossed Third Avenue, walked slowly toward Lexington. Four-story townhouses lined both sides of the street; cars were parked solid in two neat rows. Midday strollers gave him the eye. He was getting plenty of notice, none of it favorable. His clothes were wrinkled and torn, his hair was matted, and he needed a shave. Only a matter of time before a prowl car happened by and he got the bum's rush.

What was he looking for?

He'd almost reached the end of the block when he saw it. The third house from the corner. A brownstone just like all the others. Nothing to set it apart, make it distinct, except for one small item: *The room he'd been seeing in his mind's eye, the one that kept turning up again and again, was in that house. Fourth floor rear. Apartment 4B. He was absolutely certain.*

He stood frozen, his mouth half open, staring at the building. He could feel the sweat sliding down his forehead. He was dizzy, could hear his heart pounding. He had to be right. *But was he?*

Three stone steps led up to the front door. He went with them; tried the knob. Locked. He peered through the door's small window. The mailboxes were in the west wall, each with a name in its slot. But he was too far away to make out what they were. His eyes hunted for a bell, found one. *Only one?* It wouldn't do, he needed a specific bell—4B. His only chance was to buzz someone who might know him. He'd never get past the hallway if a stranger answered his ring.

He stepped back uncertainly, not sure what to do next. On the street, two men and a woman had stopped to watch him. Others were turning their heads. Another minute and he'd have a crowd cheering him on. His finger went to the bell, pressed hard. A moment and the inner door opened. A plump, middle-aged woman appeared in the alcove, looked at him through the small window. She didn't open the outer door. Block wrapped his knuckles against the glass; his lips formed the word "please."

The woman scowled, wrinkled her nose as if she could actually smell him. Abruptly, she turned on her heal; the inner door slammed shut.

Slowly Block backed down the three steps. His palms were wet, clammy; his legs felt as if someone had severed them from his body. He'd collected another five onlookers; they made way for him, disgust clear on their faces.

He headed for Lexington Avenue, turned the corner. He couldn't really blame the lady; he'd have done the same in her shoes.

Block shuffled along bleary-eyed and tired. Lexington Avenue was full of shoppers, cars, buses, noise and bustle. No place to settle down for a while, take a breather. Not the best spot for a handout either; the crowd was moving too fast.

He turned his footsteps west, in the direction of Fifth Avenue and Central Park. At least there'd be benches. People in the park wouldn't be in so much of a rush, might take time to come up with a coin or two. And the cops let you alone in the park.

If he could only remember who lived in 4B, it would make things a lot simpler. Why was it so hard? He thought back to the good old days before he'd started hitting the bottle. The early years were all right. He saw his mom and dad, plain as day, just as if they were still alive. There was the tenement house in Brooklyn. Grade school had only been a couple of blocks away. High school was somewhere else. He'd gone to college, too, but that was even harder to remember. He saw a youngish version of himself in sweater and jeans burning the midnight oil over a textbook. No use trying to square this kid with what he'd become, and Block didn't try. After that things became a blur. There were faces, all right, but each melted into another as though they were made of soft, pliable wax. In his mind he saw figures moving against the familiar backdrop of cheerful rooms, crowded streets, tall buildings. They might've been wind-up dolls on some tabletop for all the sense he could make of them.

He stopped trying to dredge up the dead past. He'd been so busy worrying where his next drink was coming from that he hadn't taken stock, hadn't realized that he'd gone off the deep end. How long had he been on this bender, anyway? What had he done to himself?

Block stood blinking, slowly looking around as if he'd just crawled out of a manhole into daylight. He was on Madison Avenue and Seventy-eighth Street. Cars, buses filled the street. Small shops — a bookstore, a high-class grocery, an art gallery — displayed their wares through shiny plate-glass windows; well-dressed men and women hustled along in all directions. Some of them stared at him, others averted their eyes. He was a stand-out, all right; he didn't belong in this part of town. But once he'd been a charter member, as upstanding as any of them.

What had happened?

Block started walking again, slowly, tried to brush the cobwebs from his mind. There was only a jibbering confusion, a mishmash of disjointed scenes. Behind it all he saw the image of the thin-lipped, flat-nosed, flicker man again. Block gave it up. He needed food, rest, he needed someone to help him. Only who?

Maybe whoever lived on the fourth floor.

— CHAPTER —
Twenty-One

We plunged down the stairs.

The girl said, "What of the prisoners on the upper levels?"

"There's a limit to this humanitarian angle," I told her. "And we've probably reached it."

Bar said, "They are safer in their cells."

Lix-el said, "How did you know about me? Is there talk that the Prime Minister of Ardenya has been illegally imprisoned here? Is that it, young man?"

"There may have been talk, but it never reached me or my digger."

"A cyborg?" Lix-el seemed shocked. "Those are run by Blanks."

I gave him a yes.

"But you, sir, are hardly a Blank."

"Right again. They tripped up somewhere."

"Indeed."

The girl said, "You are well informed on this topic."

"I am well informed on many topics, my dear."

Ganz said, "The Prime Minister led the government of Ardenya for many years. Ardenya is one of the advanced worlds."

"You know of my world, sir?"

"I do now. The facts were in your mind, my friend."

"Disgusting habit," Lix-el said, "prying into a man's mind."

"Perhaps," Ganz said, "but the habit, as you call it, does account for your being here with us, does it not?"

"I'm not complaining, sir. What is your world?"

"Qualgin."

"Hmmmm. Doesn't have a familiar ring to it," the Prime Minister said. "Most peculiar. Where is it?"

"The far end of the galaxy," I heard myself say.

"The *what?*"

"The northwest sector." I reeled off the co-ords. "Right?" I asked Ganz.

"Quite."

"This is remarkable," Lix-el said. "I thought I knew them all."

"There are hundreds," the girl said, "are there not?"

"Not of the human sort," Lix-el said. "It is my job to know them."

Bar addressed me. "You are an astronomer?" His deep voice seemed to fill the staircase.

"I'm a Blank," I told him.

"You can't be," Bar said.

"Hardly," Lix-el agreed.

The girl turned to Ganz. "Can you see into his mind?"

I said, "Yeah. Why not? Give it a try."

Ganz said, "I have already looked. Your mind is a chaos."

"Hell," I complained, "I could've told you that."

"You fail to comprehend, my friend. The process which occurs in the erasure chamber does in fact leave the mind a blank. Except for minimal instructions — work and self-care; these are imprinted on the Blank mind."

"So?"

"Gazing into such a mind, one finds a wasteland."

"I know what you mean," I told him, "but that doesn't help much."

Lix-el broke in. "Come, come, all this may be very informative — but *where* are we, and what *is* happening outside?"

Ganz smiled. "Have no fear. I have kept track. We are approaching the ninth level. Outside the battle rages. There is a weapons room in the basements. Some of the orderlies knew of it. The door has been battered down, the weapons distributed to the maties. The battle, however, is still not being fought on equal terms; it can end in but one way. Yet for the time being the prisoners hold the line. They control the courtyard. The guards are massing for an attack. It should be costly to both sides. Presently reinforcements will arrive. They should be of sufficient strength to put an end to these festivities. Satisfied?"

Lix-el nodded.

"It seems," Bar said, "that we are bottled in."

"Perhaps," Ganz said. "We shall see. I probe the minds of

the guard captains as they prepare for combat. It is their duty to foresee all contingencies however remote. In their minds there arise a variety of catastrophes—ways in which some maties might conceivably escape."

"Come up with anything?" I asked.

"So far," Ganz said, "they have small ground for worry."

We reached ground level, halted.

I doused the light. The sudden darkness seemed to close in on us. Traipsing down the stairs had at least seemed like progress, had given us something to do. Now my optimism was draining away—when I needed it most. We were as caged in here as any of the maties. Their mass exodus had seemed like a dandy idea, had created plenty of confusion. But the guards circling the prison weren't part of my scheme.

I fumbled for the girl's hand. Her fingers closed over mine. If this was it, if I was checking out for keeps, at least I wasn't going as a mindless Blank chained to a digger. The thought didn't give me much comfort.

Sounds—muffled and distorted by prison walls—reached us from outdoors.

They weren't nice sounds.

Guns boomed, blasted, crackled and rattled. Guards and maties yelled, shrieked and screamed. Outside was no place to be. Inside in a short while wouldn't be a lot better.

"Anything?" Bar rumbled; he seemed calm enough.

"No," Ganz said.

I asked, "Is it as bad as it sounds?"

"Worse."

I shifted from foot to foot. I was itching to go some-where—anywhere.

Ganz said, "We are not alone here."

"Guards?" Bar murmured.

"Maties. A group is searching the basement and sub-basement. Their mood is ugly."

"Can't very well blame them," Lix-el said.

"I believe we shall soon have even more company," Ganz said. "From the top levels. There is a cell block reserved for orderlies; their cells are more comfortable than the run of the mill and not made of metal. One of the maties has partially dismantled a door; he will presently emerge in the hallway; he is bent on freeing the other prisoners. When he does there will be hundreds heading down this very staircase."

"Just great," I complained. I was surprised to hear the bitterness in my voice.

Ganz turned to me. "About you, my nameless friend—"

"I thought you'd finished with me."

"Not quite. Your mind is unique, at least in my experience. It is a chaos of facts, figures, images."

"So you said."

"But that is not its outstanding feature."

"There's more?"

"Assuredly. There is a wall, a barrier, even I cannot penetrate." Ganz hesitated. "Come, it is time to move."

"You have spotted a way out, sir?" Lix-el said.

"Yes."

"Some guard captain," I said, "had a bright idea?"

"Not quite. The idea, my friend, came from you."

— CHAPTER —

Twenty-Two

Block sat on a Central Park bench, staring dully at the West Side skyline. Slowly he glanced around. A stout guy was flying a red kite out on the large oval field. Some kids were playing baseball. More than a few casual strollers. A lot of oldsters holding down park benches, looking about as spry as he felt. He should've gotten up, started making the rounds, palm outstretched, but he didn't have the strength. Maybe later. His eyelids had grown so heavy. . . .

Block was at the car's wheel, Professor Pavel and his daughter Anna next to him. He stared out at the snow-covered streets. A cold wind had frosted the windshield, making the night seem gray and distant. The heater was up full, but Block shivered anyway. Winter had come early, overnight, in midfall.

His headlights pointed away from the city; the tall buildings slowly vanished, snow-topped trees took their place.

Anna said, "I am uneasy." Her voice was deep, with just the hint of an accent.

Block's eyes left the highway for an instant, stared at her. She had black hair, olive skin, was in her twenties; her eyes were dark gray.

"Nothing to worry about," Block said.

Professor Pavel said, "I am not so sure."

"No maybes about it," Block said.

The professor shook his head. He was somewhere in his sixties; his face long, lips full, hair gray. His accent was more pronounced than the woman's.

"You do not understand, Mr. Block," he said.

"What's to understand?"

"Should Mr. Hastings discover what we are doing, it would be very bad for us."

"He would kill us," Anna said.

"As he killed your friend Mr. Nash," the professor said.

"Nash wasn't my friend," Block said. "And no one's killing anyone. All this is just guesswork. Let's wait till we come up with something definite before we start sweating. Relax. Enjoy the ride."

"It is easy for you to say," Anna complained, "you are merely . . ."

The flickers came.

"Yes," Anna said, "information."

"More wine?" Block asked.

"No. This is sufficient."

They were in a small midtown restaurant, in the back room, near the wall. It was dim here. And Block could watch the doorway.

"You were saying?" he said.

"Marty Nash was never in the office, Mr. Block. But he was employed by McCoy Imports."

"You saw him?"

"Twice."

"That's hardly conclusive."

"Before he retired," Anna said, "my father worked twelve years for the firm."

"*He* knew him?"

"Yes."

"Tell me a little about your father, Miss Pavel."

She shrugged. "What is there to tell? He was a professor of Slavic languages in Hungary. When he came to America he taught at numerous colleges, but found he could earn more in private industry. A colleague of his had worked for McCoy—Professor Benish—and when he retired, my father took his place."

"Your father did what?"

"European contracts. His fluency in twelve languages proved most useful."

"He had the run of the place?"

"Yes. He was a vice-president, one of twelve."

"He had access to the firm's records?"

"Of course."

"Maybe we should go have a chat with your father. . . ."

The flickers came.

The phone rang on Block's desk. He reached for it. "Yes."

"My name is Anna Pavel, Mr. Block. I work for McCoy Imports. I would like to meet with you after work. Tonight."

"Why, Miss Pavel?"

"You were inquiring about a Martin Nash this morning, were you not?"

"Yes."

"Our Mr. Hastings' secretary said no such person had ever worked for McCoy."

"That's right."

"He was lying."

The flickers came.

They had left the main highway. A narrow, snow-covered road led up a shallow hill. The going was rougher here, the car crawled along. Its headlights picked out more snow and trees; there was nothing else.

They came to an open gate, rode through, coasted down a driveway.

The house—three stories of wood and shingles—was dark.

Block pulled up in the driveway. They climbed out. The

124

snow under their feet was nearly frozen solid. A few steps had them at the door. The professor produced a key, turned it in the lock.

Inside was dark, the air stale and musty. When Pavel couldn't find the light switch, he dug a pack of matches out of a coat pocket, struck one. They were in a long, gray-walled hallway, the living room dead ahead. A staircase on the right led to the first floor; behind it was the cellar door.

They trooped into the living room. Professor Pavel lit another match, found the light switch. Pale light from a single ceiling lamp showed a pair of yellow print couches, a worn easy chair, a fireplace with a large mirror over it. Wind rattled at the windows, as though an uninvited guest were desperately trying to get in. The place was frigid.

The professor stood in hat and coat, hands jammed into pockets, slowly staring around the room.

"It is as I remember it," he said.

"What makes you think," Block asked, "that we'll find anything here?"

"This was a place Hastings knew nothing about. Of this I am sure. Nash kept it a secret."

"And you tailed him here?"

"I did. I was by then convinced, Mr. Block, that McCoy was engaged in vast illegal activities. And that Martin Nash—the *silent* partner, as it were—was at the center of these crimes. I returned with a number of passkeys. One fit. It was my intention to search this house, but a few moments here alone changed my mind. I am not—how do you call it?—a good private eye."

"Maybe we should start looking around," Block said.

"Yes," Anna said. "I do not like this place at all; it is—"

The woman broke off, stared at the hallway.

Block turned to look.

There were three of them.

The first was tall, thin, with bushy yellow eyebrows and a long cleft chin. He wore a peaked cap, long tweed coat, black muffler and gloves. The gun had a long-barreled silencer on it.

The pair behind him were half hidden by darkness. Block made out a heavyset man in a green parka; the hood all but covered his face. He glimpsed red hair, a large crooked nose, a jutting chin. The third party was short, round-shouldered, wore a leather jacket and a wide-brimmed hat pulled low. As far as Block could tell, they were all strangers to him.

The tall man raised his gun.

Block began very slowly reaching for a vase on the end table.

Pavel shot through his coat pocket.

The heavyset man sailed backward, as though caught by an invisible wave.

Peaked cap's gun jumped once in his hand.

Pavel spun sideways as if a giant finger had poked him in the ribs; he fell down. He didn't get up.

Block's hand had reached the vase. He chucked it at the overhead light, rolled off the couch. Darkness came.

Anna screamed. Block didn't know if he actually heard the soft whoosh of the silencer or imagined it. No matter. The woman was suddenly quiet. Something heavy landed on the floor.

Block cursed under his breath. Lights were apt to snap on any second. He was a sitting duck. Doubled over, almost touching the floor, Block headed for what he hoped was the hallway leading out.

Someone's stomach got in the way.

Hands — large and powerful — groped for him.

He slipped sideways, bumped into a second man.

Arms grabbed him from behind; Block put an elbow into a stomach, shook loose. Feet tripped him. Block went down. Someone landed on top of him. He kicked out, got hit in the forehead, crawled over a squirming body, pried loose a couple of fingers from his hair. For a second he was free. A second was all he needed. Block crept away, banged head first into the staircase, detoured around it, touched the cellar door, got it open and closed behind him. The handrail guided him down in stony darkness.

He reached bottom, moved away from the staircase, stopped and listened. Nothing to hear, only his own rapid breathing. The shock hit him then. Before he had been too busy fighting for his life. Now his legs almost gave under him; his mouth went dry and he thought he was going to pass out.

He managed to light a match with shaking fingers, looked

126

around. He saw a boiler, some pipes, stacked lumber. A few lone tools hung from hooks on the far wall. No door led outside. The windows were small and high up near the ceiling. He was trapped.

Block made it to the wall, reached for the hammer. Not much of a weapon, but better than nothing.

His fingers had closed around the handle when he heard the sound: a rumbling deep inside the wall.

His match flickered out. He lit another.

Part of the wall he saw, to his amazement, had slid back. Another room lay beyond.

Ross Block stepped over the threshold and the wall snapped shut behind him.

— CHAPTER —
Twenty-Three

There were six of them in my circle of light.

Ganz had pinpointed their location in the subbasement. Maties like us, hunting for a way out.

We'd done our bit for the matie cause, sent them off to the slaughter. This crew was just a nuisance. We needed privacy now.

Bar launched himself at our finds. I was going to join the fracas too. Bar banged some heads together, tossed some bodies against the wall, threw his large fists into a couple of faces. And it was all over.

I shone my light down on the floor. A heap of maties lay peaceably at the big man's feet. I spent only an instant admiring this feat.

We went by a stalled speed-lift. The door next to it was made of wood. Bar pulled it off its hinges.

We went down a ramp.

A large plush tunnel waited for us at the bottom.

We trooped through it.

Overhead, I knew, was the prison yard; it didn't take much imagination to figure what was going on up there. I was thankful to be in a safe, clean-smelling tunnel. My glower showed a thick rug underfoot. Very thoughtful. The walls were freshly painted, too. I was going to miss this place when we left it.

Our jaunt didn't last long. We came to another ramp, went up.

We were in a large garage. It smelled of fuel, oil, plasto-deck, alloy. It held three sleek, shiny, six-wheeled ground cars.

Ganz smiled at me. "See what you had in your mind?"

I almost blushed. It came back to me, all right. What the telepath had pulled out of my think-tank was something that'd been there all along—glimpsed—on one of the printouts, but not noted: the chief warders' garage and the connecting tunnel that let the brass avoid hiking through the prison yard.

"We're outside the walls," I said. "Aren't we?"

"Very good," Ganz said. "Yes, the fighting is behind us. But all roads have been blocked leading away from here. We shall have a most difficult journey."

I asked, "Know where we're going?"

"But of course. Your hovercraft."

Bar slid back the double doors.

Cool air and night greeted us.

And the sounds of combat in full swing.

The girl and I scrambled into one car, Bar, Ganz and Lix-el into another.

We rolled.

Ganz was in front running interference. If trouble popped up ahead, he would know it, steer us clear of it. Trees were on either side of the roadway. The sounds of battle gone. If anyone had seen us leave, he hadn't made any fuss about it.

The girl said, "Ganz knows where the craft is hidden?"

"He seems to think so."

"You suppose they are all like that on his world?"

"Mindreaders? Beats me."

Something clicked in my mind. I knew—suddenly—that Ganz's world wasn't populated by telepaths. I didn't bother sharing this news with the girl. I was going to keep mum till I figured out where all this stuff was coming from. If I'd been an Overseer, this was no time to advertise the fact.

The car up ahead slowed, pulled to a stop.

I jerked the stop lever, came to a standstill.

Our trio were busy jumping out of their car.

I got my door open, had one foot on the ground, when Bar waved me back. He and Lix-el came running toward us.

Ganz, only half out of the car, seemed to be waiting for something.

Bar was the first to reach us. He opened the back door, started to climb in.

"What the hell is it?" I yelled.

"There's a—"

The car up front—driverless now—had jumped ahead. It ran down the road in darkness, its lights off.

Lix-el tumbled into the back seat next to Bar. "Douse your lights," he yelled.

Ganz, I saw, was headed for us too, now. Some party.

I doused my lights.

A pair of headlights shone in the distance, grew brighter, closer—an oncoming car.

Ganz shoved in next to the girl, said one word: "Petrol."

Ahead the headlights vanished for an instant, blotted out by the bulk of our hurtling car. They appeared again for an eyeblink as cars collided—sounding like a small clap of thunder. Both vanished in flame.

From the back seat Bar rumbled, "Get going."

I wondered if we'd be able to get by the burning wrecks. I didn't get a chance to find out. As I reached for the go lever, Ganz said, "It won't do. There are more coming."

"How many?" Bar asked.

"Two ground cars."

"We must turn," Lix-el said. "Go back, find another route."

"No good," Ganz said calmly. "We are on a side road now, one that is little used. The main highways are clogged with troop movements. We would have little chance. If we can keep to this road it will lead us close to the hovercraft."

"You've got it down pat," I said.

"The maps were in your mind."

"We must destroy those two cars," Bar said. "There is no other way."

I thought it over. He might be right at that. We had more than enough guns for the job. But I wasn't too crazy about a shootout. Even with Ganz calling the shots and the element of surprise on our side, there was no guarantee we'd come out on top. Hiding out in the woods till danger passed was a much safer proposition. One glance was enough to show me that we'd never get our car off the road; the trees were too dense.

"They are coming," Ganz said.

The girl had charge of the extra guns. She passed them out.

"How much time?" I said.

"Not much," Ganz said.

Bar rumbled, "Drive this car across the roadway. It will stop them if they manage to get by the blaze."

I followed instructions; there was sense in them.

We climbed out, headed for the wreck. Heat scorched us as we ran by. We didn't give the cars a second glance—there could be no survivors.

The girl and I ran to the right. The rest scurried left.

We hid behind trees and waited.

It took longer than expected.

I lay on the ground fidgeting, smelling earth, vegetation, leaves. None of this felt as if it was happening to me. I wasn't even sure who me was: the digger Blank, the gladiator, or the man with the click mind. One thing was sure—it had been so long since I'd noticed a leaf, I'd all but forgotten what it smelled like. The thought didn't cheer me. I stretched out an arm, clasped the girl's hand. In my other hand I held a gun, a long-nosed laser. We lay that way waiting for something to happen.

I was beginning to think Ganz had been off base when headlights showed themselves down the road.

I let go of the girl's hand, gave my attention to the approaching cars. They were coming on fast. I couldn't see inside, but they had to be packed with soldiers.

The fire brought both cars up short, wheels squealing, one behind the other.

Car doors opened, men poured out; all wore uniforms, all carried guns.

There were eight altogether; none had remained behind.

They moved toward the flames. They didn't show much interest in their surroundings. We were too far from the prison for them to expect trouble.

I held my fire. So did the trio across from us. This bunch were out to inspect the crash. Each step took them farther away from their cars.

That gave me an idea.

I put my mouth against the girl's ear, whispered, "Keep your eye on them. But don't shoot till our boys open up. Work your way over to their cars. Quietly."

The girl nodded, crawled off between the trees.

I followed on hands and knees. The troops were busy poking around the fire.

That our side hadn't started blasting yet encouraged me. I began to think I might be in luck.

We had all but reached the first car when one of the soldiers noticed our six-wheeler—on the other side of the wreckage—parked lengthwise, across the roadway. He let out a holler that brought the others running.

Any second now this bunch was going to catch on they weren't alone out here.

"Okay," I whispered at the girl, "make for the second car—quick!"

She dutifully sprang to her feet, sprinted for the vehicle.

Across the road three shapes darted out of the darkness, ran for the car, too.

By now, the troops had seen us.

I aimed a laser in their direction. Bar used a blaster. There was plenty of racket.

The soldiers dived for cover; we dived for their car.

So far not a shot had been fired at us. I liked that.

I found myself behind the wheel. The rest of the gang half in, half out, popping shots at the enemy.

I didn't wait for any encouragement. My hand lunged for the go lever. The car lurched under us. I twisted the wheel, made a U-turn.

Four guns burned holes in the other car, the one we'd left behind us to act as our shield.

It blew up.

We rode away from there.

Shots sounded behind us.

I let the car out another notch. Shots, soldiers and burning cars dwindled. We turned a bend in the road and were alone again.

"Are we safe now?" the girl asked.

We rode up a small hill. For an instant the trees fell away. We could see part of the zone. Five patches of flame flickered and blazed, made the night bright. Two of the patches were sending long red fingers out toward each other.

"For the moment," Ganz said.

"You see that far, do you?" Lix-el said.

A grin crossed Ganz's long face. "My range is quite widespread."

The girl turned to me. "You counted on that."

"Yep. I figured it was better to run out on the troops than have a small war. Less chancy. That's why I held my fire, made for their cars. Smart but futile if Ganz hadn't been checking up on us. I was betting he would."

"You won your bet," Ganz said.

We parked. Climbed out. Lix-el stretched.

"Where the hell are we?" I asked.

Ganz pointed toward the woods. "The hovercraft lies through there."

We set out through the woods. The noises of havoc reached us from far off; they were very faint: shouts, the grind of equipment, vehicles on the move. I could smell smoke.

I played my glower on the ground. There was no path. We crunched on leaves and twigs. There were other movements in the woods, animals, probably; I ignored them. If Ganz wasn't worried, neither was I.

The hovercraft was still buried under shrubbery.

Ganz checked out its interior from a distance.

"Empty."

"Anyone outside?" I asked.

"No one is in this area now. They are all fighting the flames."

We tumbled into the craft. A tight squeeze, but no one was complaining. I sat at the controls, feeling right at home.

"All set?" I asked.

Four voices assured me they were. I believed them.

I pulled back on the starter.

We rose.

Twenty-Four

Block opened his eyes.

He was on his Central Park bench. The fat guy with the kite was gone. The kids were still playing baseball. The sun had moved westward, hung over the tall buildings beyond the park on Manhattan's West Side.

What'd he been dreaming of? The flickers had come again, that was it. But like nothing he'd ever seen before. Something about a professor and his daughter. Block didn't know any professors, had never been to the house in the country, knew nothing about an attack. The whole thing made no sense. Too much whiskey had rotted his mind. He was going bananas.

He remembered the brownstone; that at least rang a bell, might lead to something.

He looked around. The park was still full of people, the benches occupied; time to make a buck, maybe.

It took a couple of hours. But Block did better than he expected. Three-sixty in coins jangled in his pocket as he left the park. He was dying for a drink. The sweat coating his body had nothing to do with the weather. But if he gave in he was done for. What he really needed was chow. Knobby's ninety cents hadn't lasted long. He was past the stage where a full stomach would set things right. But without something under his belt he had no chance at all.

Block headed back toward Madison Avenue, bought coffee and a ham sandwich at a take-out shop, shuffled off with his dinner, downing it as he went. It didn't taste like much. But maybe it'd keep him going for a while; that's all he wanted.

Block made his way to Lexington Avenue.

A large clock in a bakery told him it was five-twenty. From where he stood on the corner of Lexington, he could see the house on Seventy-eighth Street. Between now and nightfall the nine-to-fivers would be drifting back home. The old biddy who'd given him the brush-off had meant nothing to him. But that left a houseful of tenants. With a little luck he'd spot one he knew. It wouldn't take much to fill in the missing pieces of his life—at least some of them. And maybe he'd even get a hand up the ladder. It was worth a try. He had nothing else going for him.

The shadows had lengthened as the sun sank behind the West Side's tall apartment buildings. A chill wind filled the air.

So far his vigil had hardly set the world on fire. A small, elderly woman had been the first to arrive. As far as he knew, he'd never seen her before. A young kid about twenty-three was next. He had long blond hair down to his shoulders and wore a black leather jacket. Scratch two. A stocky, middle-aged man with not much hair and a double chin was third. He had on a gray business suit and carried a briefcase. He looked like a hundred other guys, Block thought, and each of them was a stranger to him.

A youngish brunette went up the three stone steps. A middle-aged couple followed her. The blond-headed kid left the house. A tall guy with a beard and mustache entered it. A very fat woman showed up around seven. It was dark by then. And cold. Block had managed to attract the attention of some storekeepers. A prowl car had cruised by twice. It was only a matter of time before they gave him the heave-ho. The house, meanwhile, had filled up nicely with people. And if Block had ever laid eyes on any of them, it was news to him.

Lights were on in most of the windows. The house looked a hell of a lot cozier than a city street, Block thought, but did he really have any ties to the place? He'd been sure at first, but maybe it was all a pipe dream like pink elephants or snakes, or the dream about the professor.

How could he tell?

He'd flunked his own test. None of the tenants was in the least familiar.

Maybe the best thing to do was toss in the sponge, just keep walking.

Only where?

His future looked as bleak as his present. He didn't need a guy with a gun to finish him off. The way he was living would do the trick in no time.

Unless he did something!

He couldn't pass up *any* chance—even the slimmest—to get back on his feet. Somehow he had to find out who lived in 4B. Risks didn't matter. What could happen to him that would be worse than *this*? He had nothing to lose. Even a stretch in the pen might be an improvement.

He left the neighborhood. No profit hanging around where he'd be an eyesore. He drifted east, then north. The streets began to change. The smart little shops of Madison Avenue gave way to more practical fare. The tall buildings lost their doormen and small tenements crept in between the high-rises. He went down to First Avenue in the low nineties and almost felt at home. A tired collection of dilapidated peeling houses lined both sides of the block. As if somehow this section had been bypassed by progress. The cops wouldn't think twice about seeing him here.

He needed the breather. His strength—what was left of it—was going fast. He had no reserves to draw on. It was tough just ambling along. He'd never make it back to Seventy-eighth Street, let alone do what had to be done, if he didn't get some rest.

He was on Ninety-fourth now. Only eight-thirty, but the block had already shut down for the night. An old couple were out on the street, but they didn't give him a second glance. Some of the windows were lit up. Cracked ceilings and chipped walls were visible in the pale light. No curtains, only soiled window shades. Not quite skid row—he was the expert on that—but one hell of a way from Lexington Avenue in the Seventies.

Block curled up in an empty doorway and went to sleep.

The flickers were faded now as if coming from a great distance. Professor Pavel puffed on his pipe, smiled at Ross Block. "I am convinced," he said, "that Hastings and Martin Nash are at the center of a worldwide conspiracy."

Anna nodded.

Block shifted in his easy chair. "You have evidence, professor?"

"I have copies of documents. Huge outlays of money have made their way across borders, Mr. Block, to bribe officials, to ensure favorite treatment for McCoy Imports."

"Where does McCoy figure in all this?"

"McCoy?" The professor looked puzzled. "McCoy has been dead for thirty years, Mr. Block. Hastings is McCoy. He and the board of directors. They also hold much of the stock."

"But not all?"

"No. There are others who control the company, but they have remained in the background. My best efforts have failed to reveal their identities."

The mob, Block thought; he said, "Have anything else?"

"Yes. This Nash, Mr. Block, lived at numerous addresses, a man with something to hide. He kept one such place completely secret. I can take you to it."

Block said, "Ever meet Hastings' wife, Sally?"

The professor shook his head. "I do not think so."

"She's a blonde. Kind of plump."

"No."

"How about Nick Siscoe? Sally was married to him before Hastings."

The professor nodded slowly. "He was Nash's friend. I remember him well."

"Worked for McCoy?"

"Of course."

The flickers faded.

He awoke slowly, every part of his body aching. The damn flickers. The booze had turned his brain to total mush. Again that professor and his daughter. And some cock-and-bull story. Where did he get this crap? He didn't know, didn't care. He couldn't tell how long he'd slept. Shit! He managed to get to his feet. The flickers receded to the back of his mind. He had other things to worry about. He'd started walking back toward Seventy-eighth Street. Still very dark. He'd been lucky, could've slept right through till morning. And that would've screwed up the works. He needed darkness. And another day's wait was too long. But how much time did he have left? A clock in a darkened Chinese laundry made it three-fifteen. Not bad. A good three hours. The night was holding up, but would he?

Seventy-eighth Street was dark, deserted. He circled the block hunting for an alley, found one on Seventy-seventh Street off Third. The brownstones, all residential dwellings, were packed tight—no way to get into a backyard. But here, at the rear of a restaurant, was just what the doctor ordered.

The alley was narrow, dark. Block felt his way blindly, fingers scratching along the brick wall, feet taking small shuffling steps as if old age had set in on top of his other troubles. He bumped into some trash cans, then hit a high wooden fence. End of the line.

He went back, emptied three of the cans, carted them over to the fence. He jammed one, bottoms up, into the other, making a five-foot column. He turned the third can upside down, climbed on top, braced himself against the fence, then pulled himself up onto the other cans. Block tottered dizzily. The fence was a seven-footer, but was now only waist-high on him. He was in no shape for gymnastics. But if he couldn't swing this, how was he going to handle the really tough stuff later on? Block managed to get both legs over and dropped to the other side. He landed on soft earth, lay there, the wind knocked out of him, watching the darkness spin.

After a while things quieted down and he got back on his feet. He wasn't feeling any too spry. Part of him wondered why he didn't call it quits while he was still in one piece. The rest of him went off in search of the house he needed.

For once it was easy going. Some of the backyards had no fences at all; the rest were mostly waist-high or shorter. Even so, Block was huffing and puffing by the time he reached the brownstone.

Easy going ended right there.

He stood looking up at the third house from the corner. Like all the others, it had a fire escape in back. He'd counted on that. What he'd forgotten was that the fire escapes would all be a uniform twelve feet off the ground. Even in peak condition, he couldn't've managed it.

He tried the back door just for kicks. It didn't give an

inch. Fiddling with the ground-floor windows was too chancy; he'd land in someone's bedroom and all hell would break loose.

Retracing his steps along the backyards, Block went looking for some implement—a ladder maybe—that might do the trick. It was either that or toss in his hand. Only a sliver of moon lit his way. He climbed over the short fences, avoided the high ones, and used eyes, hands, and feet to explore the ground. If hidden treasure was buried, he failed to uncover it. Only weeds, stones and earth had been left lying around out back by the property owners of East Seventy-eighth Street. Along with a couple of knee-high picnic tables.

Block leaned up against one of the four trees decorating the backyards and tried to catch his breath. He'd blown it. There was no way he'd ever reach that fire escape. It seemed obvious, now.

But he just couldn't turn tail and call it a day. Too much future was riding on his getting up to 4B. All the future he had, in fact.

As he leaned against the tree a notion began taking shape. He left his tree for one on the far side of the yard, nine houses down. As trees went, there wasn't much to choose between them. Except this one had a couple of extras going for it: a six-foot wire fence on its right, and a fire escape not two feet away from its middle branches on the left.

The wire fence took Block a good three minutes to climb. He needed a breather when he hit the top. A thick branch was all but nudging the fence. The branch led to the tree, which led to higher branches. He had all the vim and vigor of a terminal case in the critical ward, but at least he could take his time. What else did he have to do? Block rested again, a good five minutes, before leaving the tree for the fire escape.

He made his way slowly up the cold metal rungs. Slow was the name of the game. Any faster would've shaken the fire escape, maybe alerting the good people inside. Besides, he was too feeble to put on the steam.

He had no distractions. Once he glanced down, got dizzy and decided against doing that again. The windows he passed were mostly curtained and of no interest to him anyway. Block kept his eyes fixed on the ladder and concentrated on climbing.

He reached the parapet, rolled over it and found himself on a tar roof. He lay there on his back, staring up at the sky. He wasn't sure if he'd be able to get up again. All this had made perfect sense yesterday. But now? Perfection had taken a nose dive. Two to one he'd land right in the slammer. And what for? Chances were the 4B that'd been spinning through his skull was somewhere else. On another block. Or maybe in another borough. But even if this turned out to be the right place, what would it prove? That he'd been a tenant here once? That he'd been a guest? Big deal. Whatever ties he had to this house could've ended years ago. No wonder none of the tenants he'd seen earlier had jogged his memory. To go ahead with his plan now would just be plain dumb. What he had to do was take to his heels while he still had the chance.

Only he wasn't going to do it.

He got to his feet like a pug who'd just gone ten rounds with the champ and lost them all. He began making his way over the rooftops. Parapets separated each house. He stepped over them, kept going.

He came to a halt three houses from the corner—his brownstone—surprised he'd actually gotten this far.

The roof door was locked from the inside. They usually were. So much for the easy way—there wasn't going to be one.

The fire escape was as inviting as a plot in the local cemetery. But it was the only game in town. He started down. Block was dizzy again, but not from exertion. Excitement was knocking him for a loop. His constitution wasn't used to kicks that didn't come out of a bottle.

A few steps down the ladder brought him to the right place.

Crouching on the fire escape, Block peered through the window. The blinds were up, but it still took him a while to make out the interior. He was looking into an office of some kind. He could see the desk, chair, lamp, wastebasket. They were all in place. The only thing missing was Block himself. He'd found his sunlit room. But what was he going to do with it?

— CHAPTER —
Twenty-Five

The fires burned below us.

I punched out the spaceport co-ords, took a gander at the map which had sprung up on the viewscreen. Most of our flight would be over barren terrain. We had only a couple of small cities to skirt. I settled back in the pilot's seat, gave the craft its head. The girl sat next to me.

I said, "Everyone okay back there?"

My other passengers were camped on the floor. They seemed happy enough to be there. I got a chorus of yesses.

Lix-el said, "I owe you much, sir."

"Just get me off this world," I told him, "and I'll be satisfied."

"You have a destination?"

"Haven't given it much thought. This Blank business kind of puts a crimp in your options. Know any good worlds?"

"A few."

Bar said: "If there is a price on your head, you will want to be inconspicuous."

"Price?" I said.

"The one, my friend, they offer for fugitives," Ganz said.

"Think they'll bother with us?"

"Assuredly. An escape from here will attract wide attention."

"Sorry to hear that."

"We shall become celebrities," Ganz beamed, "for as long as we survive."

The girl spoke: "This talk, it is premature. We may *never* leave this world."

"The hell we won't," I said.

"There are cities," Bar said, "and even worlds where they will never find us."

"Sounds good," I said.

"But not for you," Ganz said. "Your overriding desire, my friend, is knowledge, not safety."

"Been poking in my head again?"

"You wish to know who you are, do you not?"

"Sure."

"Then some primitive, backwater planet is not for you."

"Too bad. I just about had my heart set on a jungle hut. What have you got up your sleeve, Ganz?"

"The Control World, my friend."

Lix-el said, "The very seat of the Galactic Arm? You *can't* be serious?"

"But I am," Ganz said.

"What's so special about this Control World?" I wanted to know.

"For one, the security forces," Bar rumbled in his deep voice. "They are everywhere."

"Sounds nice," I said.

Ganz shrugged. "My friend, you have already demonstrated that you are a man of considerable talent."

"Yeah, considerable. On good days."

"But you have survived here," Ganz said, "and thus far your escape has been successful."

"So far," I said, "isn't very far."

"Further than others have ever gone," Ganz said.

"Possibly. But why the Control World?"

"Because of the towers in your mind. You do recall the towers?"

I nodded.

"And the streets beyond?"

"So?"

"That, my friend, is the Capital."

"My dear Ganz," Lix-el said, "he might have seen pictures or viewscreens of the Capital anywhere. Surely your evidence is too scanty to act upon?"

"Perhaps. But what of the palace?" Ganz asked.

"Palace?" Lix-el said.

"He sees it as a palace," Ganz said. "It is the Chairman's residence."

"Indeed?" Lix-el seemed impressed.

I turned, stared out into the darkness. The craft was running on its own better than I could ever guide it. We'd be zeroing in on the spaceport soon. Time to pull myself together, focus on what lay ahead. But my mind was back in the palace. I saw the chubby yellow-haired man again, and his circle of admirers. The towers peeked in through the wide windows. And I could feel the throbbing city beyond them. But what connection did all this have to me?

Ganz said, "Yes, my friend, you see the *interior* of the residence."

"What about it?"

"It is restricted ground. None know what the interior is like," Ganz said, "except those who have been inside and seen for themselves. And their number is quite small."

"But *you* know, sir," Lix-el said.

Ganz merely smiled.

Small pinpoints of light glistened below. We were approaching the spaceport.

Ganz spoke from behind me: "Would you mind if I took over the controls now? It might prove safer."

"You can fly this thing?"

"Assuredly."

"Then how come I'm doing all the work?"

"Work is character-building," Ganz said.

We switched places.

I crouched next to Bar and Lix-el. The craft immediately began to sink.

"We shall descend to treetop level," Ganz said. "They have spotter-rays."

I said, "You can pick out spotter-rays, too?"

"What do you take me for?" Ganz asked.

"I don't really know," I admitted.

The hovercraft leveled off. I half rose, looked over Ganz's shoulder. The ground was no more than forty feet away.

"Sit down," Ganz said. "You make me nervous."

I sat down.

Ganz said, "It is the mind of the man running the spotter that I enter."

"Just like that? From all the hundreds down there?"

"Thousands, not hundreds. I have been seeking him for some time," Ganz said. "A mind engaged in operating a spotter-ray has a unique pattern, my friend. One learns to seek out the patterns. This particular trooper is called

Jarnal. He has no inkling of our existence. I should surmise therefore that the theft of this craft has so far gone unnoticed. We are in luck."

"That's putting it mildly," I said.

"Lix-el," Ganz said, "can you pilot a jumper?"

"I have a permit for one," Lix-el said.

"It has no doubt expired by now," Ganz said. "Along with all documents attesting to your onetime citizenship."

"No doubt, sir," Lix-el said. "Why a jumper?"

"What other choice have we?" Ganz said. "We can hardly expect to make off with a spaceship and remain undetected. But who would miss a jumper?"

"Yeah," I said, "and how could you spot one in outer space?"

"Precisely," Ganz said.

"Trouble is," I said, "a long trip in one of those babies is apt to get a bit cramped."

"That, I am afraid, cannot be helped," Ganz said.

"And if we run afoul of a meteor storm . . ." Lix-el said.

"It's bye-bye us," I said.

"My friends," Ganz said, "even if we were successful in stealing a spaceship, they would soon have the entire navy pursuing us."

"Right at our heels," I said. "And with enough firepower to blast us to kingdom come."

"You know this for a fact?" Lix-el said.

"Yeah."

"What are your sources?"

"I've got a trick mind."

"Kingdom come," the girl said, "is preferable to remaining on this world."

"So it is," Bar agreed. "But we have a third way."

"It is settled," Ganz said.

"We hop a jumper," I said.

"It was never in dispute," Lix-el said.

Ganz brought the craft in without a hitch.

No searchlights probed the night sky, no sirens roused the sleeping base. We stepped out on the hard surface of a runway.

I took a deep breath. No smoke, just clean air, filled my lungs. I already had the spaceport printout in my hand.

Shielding the glower, I tried to figure where we were. "Not too bad," I said. "We're on their landing strip. The ships are parked at the other end. If we keep heading right long enough, we ought to trip over a jumper."

"We will not be given the chance," Ganz said.

"Trouble?" Bar rumbled.

"Our arrival," Ganz said, "has not gone entirely unnoticed."

"It is so quiet," the girl said.

"We tripped an infrared spotter-eye on landing," Ganz said. "The security personnel are confused. Only one signal on the alarm board blinks; the rest are dark. They believe the blinking light to be a malfunction. That, my dear, is why there are no sirens. Yet."

"The yet ruins everything," I complained.

"Perhaps. May I see your printout?"

I gave it to him. Along with the glower. I'd've given him my pants, too, if he'd asked.

I stood there, shifting from foot to foot, fingering my blaster. We were on a deserted runway, our hovercraft the only cover in sight. A hell of a place to make a last stand.

Ganz silently returned printout and glower to me, crawled back into the hovercraft. I gazed at him glumly through the open hatch. The control-panel lights had snapped on, and Ganz was busy fiddling with the autopilot. I knew the hovercraft had no chance against the hundreds of spaceport aircraft if it came to a getaway.

Ganz rejoined us. "Better stand back," he said.

The hovercraft snapped to life, its engine humming.

We got out of the way in a hurry.

It rose five feet off the ground, turned its nose southwest and buzzed off.

I watched it coast across the landing strip, till it was lost in the darkness.

"I'm glad something is trying to escape," I said, "even if it *is* only a machine."

"Watch," Ganz said.

I stared into the darkness, saw nothing, heard nothing.

"Well?"

"Patience, my friend."

I heard the crash before I saw the flames. Less spectacular

han the power station blowup, but this looked like no time
o brag.

"Security headquarters," Ganz said simply.

"Just like old times," I said. "You've taken a page from my
ook. Twice."

"I didn't think you'd mind."

"What do we do now?"

"Head in the other direction."

There was plenty of noise.

Sirens wailed, searchlights cut into the sky, bells clanged,
nd cars sped through the night. But not near us. All the
uss was going on around Security HQ. Or what was left of
t.

Only two sentries patrolled the jumper field.

They were paying more attention to the distant clamor
han to their jobs.

A mistake.

Bar charged out of the darkness, socked one in the
oodle. He went down, stayed down.

The other had his weapon half drawn. Half wasn't good
nough.

Bar flattened him with one backhand swipe.

Bar ran off into the darkness. Some Bar.

We followed.

The big man was busy inspecting jumpers when we
aught up with him. "First two seem ready to go," he
umbled at us.

"Oxygen, rations, power pack?" Ganz asked.

Bar nodded.

Ganz said, "Bar and I will take one, you three another.
You have decided on a destination?"

"The Control World," I said, "if it's okay with my friends
ere."

The girl said yes.

"It is," Lix-el said, "the place to go."

"Wait for my takeoff," Ganz said, "and follow quickly.
The spotter-ray rotates the circumference of the base. The
earchlights are more erratic. I will move when they are all
imed away from us."

We didn't waste time hustling into the jumpers.

Lix-el sat at the controls, the girl and I strapped in behind him.

We waited.

Slowly, as in a dream, Ganz's craft rose off the ground. Then darted skyward.

Lix-el pulled back on the lever.

We jumped.

The prison world was below us, a small ball growing smaller. Darkness was all around us. Stars twinkled far away. I couldn't see Ganz's jumper.

"Our partners out there?" I asked.

"Yes," Lix-el said; he pointed at a small viewscreen. "There."

A tiny dot was moving rapidly away from us.

"Are they going in the wrong direction?" I asked. "Or are we?"

"Neither," Lix-el said. "Our craft is bound for the Control World; theirs—obviously—for someplace else."

"I'll be darned," I heard myself say.

The girl said, "They did not say they would come with us."

"Yeah, there's that. But I kind of figured they would."

"It hardly matters, sir. We are free."

"Free," I said.

The girl was smiling at me.

I felt a growing elation. And a tremendous weariness. Weariness won hands down.

I put my arms around the girl and kissed her.

Then I went to sleep.

I was walking through crowded city streets. Slender metal-and-glass buildings rose toward a clear cloudless sky. I knew that somewhere in the blocks ahead I'd find the Palace of Light. I was going to do something there—something important—but I didn't know what it was. Urgency drove me on. The crowds grew denser. I began to push and shove through them. Hands started to tear at me, feet to trip me. I felt a huge weight on my back; bodies were piling on top of me, mounds of them. I sank to the pavement, which cracked under my weight. I fell through.

I was in a small, white-walled room. The crowd was gone. I was alone except for the small, chubby, blond-headed man on the table. He still wore the metal cap on his head. The machine to which he was attached was humming.

I started to move toward the table.

The short man jumped up, wild-eyed, ran out a door. I ran after him. I chased him along narrow corridors, up and down winding staircases, through cracked courtyards where weeds and grass grew between ruined blocks of concrete.

I was walking on an empty highway. As far as the eye could see to the right and left of me, green fields stretched off toward the horizon. The sun directly overhead burned down on me. I kept walking. I was hunting the small blond man.

A man stepped out from behind a tree next to the highway. He wasn't the one I sought, although I seemed to know this one too from somewhere.

He was in his late sixties, of medium height, with brown glistening eyes, black hair, shoulders too wide for his squarish body. He smiled at me, kept bowing and rubbing his hands together. We walked down the highway talking to one another. I tried to understand what he was saying — I knew it was important — but his words made no sense to me.

Far ahead of us I saw the blond man; I began to run after him. But he ran down into a valley, and when I got there I couldn't find him. I ran back, looking for the broad-shouldered man, but he was gone too.

I opened my eyes.

Lix-el was still at the jumper's controls. The girl was asleep in her seat. I shot a glance at the panel's viewscreen: empty. Ganz was really gone. And no ships were dogging us.

I'd done it, blasted my way off the Penal World. And taken a couple of maties along for the ride.

What's more, I was bound for the Control World, which according to Ganz was the setting of my dreams.

But I wasn't going there cold; I had a contact. I'd come awake with an extra piece of knowledge in my mind.

I knew the identity of the broad-shouldered man.

Twenty-Six

Block looked over his shoulder. The windows across the courtyard were all dark. No one apparently had taken notice of his jaunt over the rooftops and down the fire escape. The night belonged to him. Something a bit more tangible would've suited him better.

He turned back to the window, gave it a try. No dice. Just as well, he thought; too much of a good thing might've gone to his head.

Block stripped off his jacket, wound it around his hand. He was about to become a prime candidate for the lockup. He had no idea if anyone was asleep in the apartment. He couldn't tell how much noise he might make. For all Block knew he'd wake up the whole house. But if there was a smarter way of getting into the place, he'd missed it.

Block drove his fist through the window. Glass shattered, crashed to the floor. He'd meant to make a small hole just below the latch; instead, he'd knocked out half the window.

Block froze, held his breath waiting for the running footsteps, raised voices that were sure to follow. There was only the sound of the wind, the beating of his heart.

He pulled his hand back carefully, freed it of the jacket.

He turned the latch, raised the window, climbed over the sill. As easy as pie, Block thought, so why was he shaking?

A thick carpet lay underfoot, which had helped cushion the sound of falling glass. He stood by the window, still half sure the commotion would attract a crowd. No sounds, not even the ticking of a clock. Thick walls, thick floors, a house built long ago. He'd picked the right site to break and enter.

Crossing the room, Block opened a door, peered into a darkened bedroom. The bed was neatly made; no one was in it. He visited a small kitchen and a medium-sized living room next. A final door led out to the fourth-floor hallway. That was it — the grand tour. He went back to the office, sat down in the desk chair, swiveled to stare through the darkness at the broken window. The pose seemed familiar enough. But no new insights came with it. If this was what he'd risked his neck for, he'd been short-changed.

Block got up, pulled down the blinds, flipped the light switch. Nothing had popped up in his head that seemed especially interesting, but maybe he was hunting in the wrong place.

He pulled open the desk drawer. Sheets of paper were stacked inside; they were as blank as his prospects. A ball-point pen and some pencils added nothing to the picture. He looked under the desk blotter, in the wastebasket, and even under the rug. For all the good it did him, Block thought, he could've stayed holed up in his Ninety-fourth Street doorway and caught a few extra hours shut-eye.

He went into the kitchen, gave the fridge a try. The loaf of whole-wheat bread was hard as a rock. The peas and spinach in the freezer compartment were covered by ice. Whoever owned this joint hadn't bothered with the fridge in months.

He found some canned goods and instant coffee in the cabinet over the sink, along with a set of dishes.

The living room was a washout.

He went into the bedroom. A couple of jackets, three pairs of trousers, a suit and overcoat hung in the closet. He tried on a brown tweed jacket. A bit loose, maybe, but not a bad fit.

He wondered whose clothes these were. *His, maybe?* Now that he was here, the place didn't exactly feel like home. Maybe the guy he'd pictured at the desk wasn't him, after all. Easy come, easy go. *Only none of this had come easy.*

Suddenly he didn't care anymore. One bum more or less in the world wouldn't make much difference. He stank and itched and was good for nothing, a pure waste, if ever there was one. His mistake was in running from the flicker man; he should've let him finish the job.

Maybe he hadn't learned anything, but there was at least one way he could still put his visit here to good use. He tossed the tweed jacket onto the bed, rummaged in the dresser for socks and underwear, carried them into the bathroom.

He couldn't remember the last time he'd taken a bath or

shower, but he still knew what to do. He stripped off his tattered clothes, filled the bathtub with hot water and climbed in. He didn't know how long he soaked. After a while Block got to his feet, turned on the shower. He used plenty of soap and two washclothes. It took some doing, but he scrubbed off the dirt. A final shampoo and he was almost human. Block toweled himself dry, stepped over to the sink, frisked the medicine chest, came up with razor and shaving cream, and got busy. He broke out a new toothbrush, brushed his teeth, ran a comb through his hair, and the job was done.

Block put on the clean underwear and socks, padded back to the bedroom. He gave himself the eye in the dresser mirror. He should've looked like something the cat dug up in the backyard. He didn't. His skin was a bit too pale. And maybe he was missing ten pounds or so. But he didn't look the way he'd felt just an hour ago — as if he were on his last legs. Block couldn't figure it. But then most things in his life had stopped adding up long ago. He wasn't going to let it bother him now. He had more important things to do.

Going into the kitchen, he put some water on to boil, started opening canned goods. His appetite was still no great shakes, but he managed to polish off a good-sized helping of beets, corn, wax beans and asparagus. He ate right out of the cans and washed it down with three cups of black coffee. Then he went back to the bedroom and began trying on clothes.

Block found the two hundred bucks in a pants pocket. It was just lying there, wrapped up in a rubber band. He sat down on the bed weak-kneed and counted it again. He couldn't believe it! He was in the chips. Two hundred smackers was more than he'd seen in months, if not years. Things were finally starting to break his way. He thought of how much booze his new fortune could buy. His head was spinning. It took him a while to remember he was off the stuff — or was he?

Ross Block went back to the closet and started hunting in earnest. The folded sheet of paper had slipped through a hole in an overcoat pocket, was lodged in the lining. Block worked it back up through the coat. Four names and addresses on it — Manhattan numbers. For all he knew they could've come right out of the phonebook; they meant nothing to him. Maybe he'd gotten his wires crossed, after all, busted into the wrong place? Maybe there never had been a right place? He could hardly complain.

He didn't find anything else. That was okay with him. Why be greedy?

He finished getting dressed, settling on charcoal-gray slacks, a gray tweed jacket, a dark-blue sports shirt. He was a bit worried about the black gum-soled shoes, but they fit like a charm. Block took a look-see in the mirror. He had to grin. He was the spitting image of the average Joe. It didn't take much to change a deadbeat into a solid citizen, just some new duds.

The overcoat was too heavy. The raincoat looked about right. He kept it on. Time to go; he didn't want to push his luck. But maybe he still had a couple of minutes. Why not? He stretched out on top of the bed, sighed. A long time since he'd been in such cushy surroundings. Block closed his eyes. It was going to be only for a second.

In the flickers, Block saw the door snap shut behind him.

He lit a match.

He was in a small, cell-like room. The walls were made of concrete. No windows. An old battered trunk stood in the room.

Block lit another match, moved toward the trunk. He knew the three killers upstairs would be hunting for him; he was the only witness to their crime. His car was still parked outside, and no footprints led off in the snow. They'd ransack the house. And sooner or later hit the basement. The hammer had sprung the hidden door. Maybe he was safe here. But if they knew about the hammer trick, he was trapped for sure. Block prayed the old trunk held a weapon.

He lit a third match, lifted the creaky lid.

The trunk was empty—except for a two-by-four metal box.

Block's heart sank, but he reached for the small box; Nash might have something important stashed in it. Maybe this was the evidence he'd been hunting for. He slid back the top.

White light blinded him, seemed to stab into his brain.

He reeled backward, crashed into the wall.

White light spun around him, flickered on and off.

He had the gun in his hand, felt his finger tighten on the trigger. And knew he was smiling.

The man backed up, his hand half raised as if to ward off the shot.

The crowd screamed.

He squeezed the trigger.

The man hurtled against the wall, blood spurting from his mouth as he crumpled to the floor.

The tall thin man with the flat nose and narrow black suit stepped out of the crowd, aimed his gun at Block.

The sound of the gun blast seemed to shake the walls.

Block barely managed to flip the lid closed. He shook his head, desperately trying to clear it. The trick door, he saw, was wide open.

And two of the three killers no more than five feet away.

Block felt himself move without thinking, without knowing what he was doing. He lashed out with his foot. Peaked cap's gun flew from his hand. In the same motion, Block brought the metal box down on the smaller man's head. Gunfire cooked Block's cheek. His open palm sliced into peaked cap's neck. The tall man sat down. A right to the chin and shorty joined him.

Block ran for the stairs. He had no idea how he'd managed to flatten two armed killers in the space of five seconds. He didn't know what had caused the piercing light from the metal box. Or the crazy image of gunplay that had darted through his brain. He didn't care. Ross Block was busy running for his life.

He came awake slowly, not sure where he was. He was lying on something soft, so he couldn't be in a doorway. Where else then? Block opened his eyes.

And saw he had company.

He was tall, but stockier than peaked cap. His face had been half hooded in the new flickers. Except for the red hair, jutting chin, large crooked nose. But even without that, his height and green parka would've been a dead give-away. The professor had shot him in the old house. But here he was, up and about, and as good as new. In the flickers nothing was real. But the gun the man held seemed real enough.

Block blinked at the redhead, hoping against hope he would disappear. He didn't.

The redhead spoke through tight lips. "Where is it, palsy?"

Block managed to open his mouth. He was lucky to do even that. No words came out.

"Let's have it, palsy," the redhead said.

Block tried to wet his lips with a dry tongue. "Wh-what do you want?" he whispered.

The guy shook his head sadly. "Don't do that. Don't get wise with me. You don't want that kinda trouble. Just tell me where you got it."

Block didn't want *any* kind of trouble. His throat felt parched, his tongue swollen. Any second now he was going to break into tears. "I . . . I don't know what you mean."

"The *thing*, palsy."

"Please," Block said. "Maybe I used to know, once—"

"Whaddya mean once?"

"Before I started boozing."

"What's that got to do with anything?"

"It's screwed up my mind."

"No shit, palsy?"

"I've been sick," Block said. "I'm just a bum now. I can't remember anything."

"A bum, palsy? You don't *look* like a bum."

Block thought of his new clothes, the shave and shower. "I cleaned up."

"You did a swell job." The redhead grinned. "You remember *me* though, don't you?"

Block wanted to say no. "Yes," he heard himself whisper.

"Sure you do. And you remember what we did to your two pals?"

Block nodded weakly.

"Listen, palsy. We been watchin' this dump for a long time, waitin' for you to come back."

"Come back," Block whispered.

"Yeah. That was dumb. But you ain't so dumb you wanna die?"

"No."

"That's smart." The redhead grinned. "So cough up the little box, and maybe we forget the whole thing."

"Box?"

153

"Yeah. You had it in your mitt when you creamed Mike. *The small metal box!* Don't get me sore, palsy."

Block stared at the gunman. What could he say? That he'd only seen the box just now—in the flickers? That he didn't know where it was? That he knew almost nothing about *himself?* The redhead would never buy it.

"I . . . I . . ." Block began.

And the flat-nosed flicker man tiptoed into the room behind the redhead with a very large gun balanced in his right hand.

— CHAPTER —

Twenty-Seven

"Lix-el," I said.

The small man turned in his seat, faced me. The jumper was on auto. Unless we had to take evasive action, it would stay that way till we sighted the Control World. We had five days to go. The girl was still in dreamland.

"Sleep well?" he asked.

"Yeah. How long was I under?"

"Six hours."

"Could've used a couple more."

"By all means. I will keep watch—what little is necessary. I hardly expect them to find us out here."

"They'll get a crack at that when we hit landside," I said. "We'll be alone, isolated, on enemy ground."

Lix-el shrugged. "I have a few connections on that world, sir, a friend or two."

"Long way from home."

"A vast distance."

"But you've got an in?"

"Fortunately."

"I'll say. How come?"

"I have already told you that I was the victim of a coup. On Ardenya."

"Could happen to anyone."

"I regret that it happened to me. Should have seen it coming, sir."

"Like Ganz?"

"Hardly. No special talents were needed. The Galactic Arm did not then control my world. But they were reaching out. Our independence in the Galactic Council irked them."

I asked what happened.

"They bought my chief of staff."

"Just like that?"

"He is now Prime Minister. He and the army joined forces to overthrow me."

"Why?"

"The army has since increased its portion of the budget by thirty percent."

"Nice."

"I almost succeeded in escaping. They apprehended me at the spaceport. Then there was a staged trial, an Arm specialty; they have it down to an art."

"Threw the book at you?"

"A life sentence."

"You were lucky."

"I suppose so. It did not seem so at the time. Many of my ministers were also arrested. But some escaped. They set up a resistance movement. I was kept informed through the grapevine, while still in prison on Ardenya. My ambassador to the Control World, Fas-Ten, went underground. And some of his staff with him. He vowed to erect a clandestine network, one that might put a dent in the Galactic Arm."

"When was this?"

"Two years ago."

"And what happened?"

Lix-el smiled. "Who can say? There is no such thing as a grapevine on the Penal World. And I have been sitting there for some time. But if I were a betting man, sir, I would wager my money on Fas-Ten."

"Think you can reach him?"

"Yes, there is a contact, a manufacturer from Ardenya who emigrated to the Capital."

"Well, then it's a good thing we're both going there, isn't it? Does the name Van-See mean anything to you?"

"Should it, sir?"

"He's some kind of big shot in the Capital. I've been dreaming about him it seems, all along."

"Dreaming?"

"Yeah. And darned if his name didn't just come to me."

"Van-See."

"Yeah."

"Shouldn't be hard to locate if he's at the Capital. You believe you knew him once?"

"Before they erased me. Or why would I be dreaming of him?"

"Why indeed?"

— CHAPTER —

Twenty-Eight

The redhead saw Block's eyes widen, whirled.

Two guns went off together.

Block was off the bed and running, before the sounds had died.

He reached the other room in nothing flat.

Five steps brought him to the open window. He dived through as though crocodiles were nipping at his heels.

More shots rang out from the bedroom.

Block headed down the ladder as fast as he could. Any second now one of those guys was likely to finish off the other. And remember *him*.

He got to the first floor, released the hooks which held the last section of ladder in place and beat it down to ground level.

All these fireworks were attracting attention. Lights were snapping on, tenants sticking their heads out of windows. The cops wouldn't be far behind, either. He wasn't ready to face the cops; not with an empty head and a pocket full of someone else's money. When it came to fall guys, he was Johnny-on-the-spot.

He got through the backyards without breaking his neck, stopping just long enough to grab a small red metal picnic table someone had thoughtfully left lying around. He lugged it over to the fence, climbed on top. The shooting had stopped by now. And he was the only other victim handy. It was all the inspiration he needed. One leap had him dangling from the fence top. He hoisted himself over, hung by his hands, and dropped to the ground. His teeth rattled, but it could have been a lot worse.

He hustled out of the alley, turning east toward Third Avenue. Early morning, only a few people on the streets. In the distance he heard the sirens. For a moment he panicked, his eyes hunting for a doorway, a subway entrance where he might hide. Then it hit him. He wasn't a bum anymore. As long as his two hundred smackers held out, he was one of the gentry. Ross Block squared his shoulders, started down the street fast, just as though he really had someplace to go.

He sat at a rear table in a joint on First Avenue and Sixty-sixth Street and finished his second cup of coffee. The place was half empty, which suited him fine. Too much hustle and bustle made his head go round. He wasn't used to polite society anymore. He kept thinking the waiter would hop over any second and send him packing. Aside from that, he was holding his own. His breakfast of orange juice, pancakes with maple syrup and coffee had almost tasted like food. His stomach seemed to be taking it all in stride. And his hands only shook once in a while. Real progress if ever there was any. Too bad progress ended right there.

At least two guys had come gunning for him during the last forty-eight hours. For all he knew, a dozen more were lining up to give it a whirl. All he'd been doing lately was downing the hooch. That shouldn't have gotten anyone sore at him except, maybe, the local temperance league. But what had he been up to before that? Knocking off some guy in full view of the flicker man and a mob of howling on-lookers? Watching the redhead's pals knock off Professor Pavel and his daughter? Swiping a metal box someone wanted back? All that? *Or nothing?*

The flicker man could've been his long-lost brother, for all he knew. Or one of his bosses, or a colleague or sidekick—provided he had any of those. Or maybe the opposition, since everyone he met recently seemed to fit under that heading. *Only the opposition to what?*

Maybe it would come back to him. Maybe the answers would just pop back into his mind?

Only he couldn't wait that long. Or count on maybes.

He took out the piece of paper from his pocket, gave it a long, hard look.

Block got off the subway at the Spring Street station. The train roared off down the tunnel, leaving him alone on the platform. He made his way up into daylight.

He was back again, only a few blocks from the Bowery. But he might've been in another city. There were tenements here, too. And old factory buildings that'd been converted into lofts. The streets were anything but fancy. Comparisons ended right there. No bums filled the gutters, littered the pavements. Flophouses and dingy diners were nowhere in sight. Block was in Soho, the chic downtown art district. He headed east, past the local paperback bookshop, its windows full of garish underground journals. Ten-thirty in the morning, the streets still had an empty, washed-out look to them. Only a few pedestrians ambled along. Cars whisked by on their way to somewhere else. The crowds would come later.

Block crossed West Broadway, and there it was, the first house on the corner. A five-story walkup. Black fire escapes ran down the building's front. An old place like hundreds of others in this end of town. But no torn shades or broken windows disfigured it. Potted plants decorated the window-sills. There were blinds and curtains, and the sidewalk in front of the building had been swept. Even the trash cans were lidded. Not bad, Block thought; now if he could only figure out what he was doing here.

Craning his neck, Block gazed up at the building. If he'd ever seen it before it was news to him. He checked the address just to be sure. This was the number, all right. But so what? How did he know it had anything to do with him? His big find, the slip of paper, probably belonged to someone else, a total stranger. Nothing he'd turned up in 4B had his name on it. Even if he'd hung out there once, those days were long gone.

Yet this was his only lead.

He went into the hallway, pressed the 3D bell, wondering if anyone would be home at this hour.

A voice through the intercom said, "Yes? Who is it?"

He had his answer all ready. "Mailman. Special delivery."

The buzzer sounded and he went through the inner doorway. The three magic words had done the trick. And why not? They always got him to open his door, didn't they? Block stopped dead. For an instant he'd seen himself walking across a large, carpeted room, to answer a ring from downstairs. He was wearing a black robe over blue pajamas. The place he was in looked nothing like the apartment on East Seventy-eighth Street. He tried to think back, but the image wouldn't come again. As if a large wave had swept it clean out of his head.

Block hit the third-floor landing, went down the hallway. The door to 3D was half open. A young woman peered out from inside. She was in her late twenties, about five three, slim, with curly brown hair. Her face was oval, nose pert, lips thin. He knew the color of her eyes—brown—without looking. She squinted at him in the dim hallway. "Ross?"

The floor seemed to open up under Ross Block. He sailed down into a very dark, endless night.

— CHAPTER —

Twenty-Nine

The jumper dropped like a dead weight out of the sky.

We'd waited till night. The Control World lay below, covered by darkness. Lix-el aimed for a patch of blackness that our viewscreen told us was an empty field. The ground rose. I saw trees, houses, roads and highways on the viewscreen, and off in the distance—through our jumper window—a city.

"The Capital," Lix-el said.

"How far?"

"Five links."

The girl said, "The Data Banks are in the Capital."

"Indeed, yes," Lix-el said.

"Our files will be there."

"Right," I said. "Somewhere, probably."

"We will know who we are," the girl said, her eyes bright.

"If we can reach them."

"You will try?"

"That's the idea."

Lix-el set us down easy. The ground seemed to tilt once, right itself. The craft shuddered. And stood still.

Lix-el beamed at us. "The hand never forgets its cunning."

"How long since you've done this?" I asked.

"A good ten years, my boy."

We didn't linger in the jumper; five days in that crate were four too many. I had the hatch open in jig time. The girl was first to hit solid ground; Lix-el and I weren't far behind.

I stood there, my legs feeling weak and wobbly. The ground was firm enough, but I wasn't. I took a long breath; the air smelled okay, not like overheated metal, plasto-deck seats and recycled oxygen. I put an arm around the girl. She leaned against me.

"Here it is," I said, my voice sounding small and strange in the open air.

"It is hard to believe," she whispered.

I told her, "We may be making one big mistake coming here—you realize that?"

"I have thought of it many times."

"Messing around with the Galactic Arm can put us right back in a cell, this time for keeps. We're out now. If we lie low, keep our heads down, they might never spot us."

"But then we will not know who we are, or our names even."

"That's the price."

"It is too high."

"You sure?"

"Yes." Her voice seemed firm enough.

"Just checking," I said.

"You too wish to go on?"

"Yeah."

"Well," Lix-el said, "I'm relieved that is settled. We can't stay here all night."

"What's on the agenda?" I asked him.

"We drive the jumper into the woods."

"And then?"

"Head for the Capital, my boy."

We kept to the fields. We went up hills and down hills, across grassy clearings and through sparsely wooded terrain. After being cooped up in the jumper, stretching a leg wasn't half bad. We tried to keep some road or highway in sight. We could see cars passing by. They grew in number as we approached the city.

The Capital wasn't all slim towers and elevated walks. We hit a slum section right off that was as good as any. The streets narrow, dirty; the buildings old and decaying. It was my first sight of civilization on this world.

"My dreams didn't include this," I told the girl.

"You were fortunate."

On the streets vendors hawked their wares; music blared from open windows; gambling games pulled in the strollers.

"Safer here," I said, "than in the fields probably. We camp here till morning?"

"I think not," Lix-el said.

"What've you got in mind?"

"To make contact at once."

"*At this hour?*"

"As good a time as any."

"Know your way around this town?"

"I have been here before."

"What do we do?"

"Follow me."

"Seems simple enough."

It was a largish edifice of metal, glass and alloy. Looked to be a good hundred levels, and ran for half a block.

The streets were wide, well lit — and except for us, empty.

We stood in a doorway across from this building. I felt naked in the empty street, exposed.

"How do we get in?" I said.

"The easiest way."

We crossed the street. Nobody blew any whistles. Anything that got us out of the open was okay with me. Our lack of IDs was just one of our worries. We had no credit clips, no money of any kind. Small matters like feeding ourselves would become major problems. Lix-el scanned the tenant roster. There were a good thousand names on it.

"Anyone in particular?" I asked.

"Yes. Ken-Rue. From Ardenya. The manufacturer I spoke of."

"Going to wake him?"

"What a question."

Lix-el's finger moved to an indent, touched it.

We waited. But not for long.

An overhead viewscreen lit up. We were being given the once-over.

The door swung open. Someone upstairs had recognized Lix-el.

We stepped into a wide marble lobby, went to the speed-lift and were shot topward. We'd passed inspection.

The man who met us at the door was short and fat and wore a dressing gown over slacks and shirt. He didn't look happy.

"Come in quickly."

We didn't argue.

Inside was a spacious living room full of fancy furniture, doodads and artwork. A tall man with mustache and pointed chin was there, too.

I was all set to slide my gun loose when Lix-el said, "Fas-Ten!"

I eased up. This Fas-Ten was the ex-ambassador we'd come to find. Only his being here seemed to be stretching luck a bit too far.

"Thank goodness you had the sense to come directly here," Fas-Ten said. "The whole planet is hunting for you!"

I sank into an overstuffed red-and-gold armchair; the girl took its twin across the room. Our host went away to fix us some food. Lix-el and his ambassador paced back and forth talking in low voices. That was okay with me. I was willing to let the former Prime Minister carry the ball. At least he knew his way around this world.

I stretched out my legs, sighed, grinned at the girl and turned my head to gaze out at the city through the glass wall. We were on the eighty-ninth level.

And got a surprise.

The angle was different, but that didn't mean anything. My towers were out there, all of them, the same tall, graceful structures I'd seen so often—in my dream.

Something went click.

I could see the Capital Building. I was inside it. I had been there many times before. I went to a window, looked out. The same towers again. Only the view still wasn't right. I corrected for it. I was some half link away. The room was large, the windows wide, the floors highly polished and gleaming. This was my Palace of Light. But it wasn't a palace. It was the Chairman's personal residence, just as Ganz had said. I strode to a window, glanced out. The towers looked back at me, each in its right place now.

I shook my head. And the picture faded. The girl was still seated across from me. Lix-el and Fas-Ten were still chatting away. Nothing had changed. *Except me.*

I closed my eyes, tried to figure out what was going on. Seeing the towers had triggered something in my mind, uncovered a memory hidden there.

I knew what had to be done now.

"Gentlemen," I said.

My voice must have had an edge to it. Both men turned.

"What is it?" Lix-el said.

"I think," I said, "it's time you counted us in."

"We were discussing our situation," Fas-Ten said irritably. "There is more involved here than the fate of a few individuals."

The girl spoke from across the room. "We have a right to know what has occurred."

Fas-Ten's face was grayish. "There is a planetwide alert for all of you."

"Just us three?" I said.

"It is for five."

"That's better."

The girl asked, "They have beamed our pictures?"

"Only on the security channel. It is closed."

"But not to you," I said.

Fas-Ten turned to his fellow countryman. "Who is this man?"

"He made possible my escape," Lix-el said.

"He *knows* of our movement?"

"I told him."

"That was not wise."

I grinned at him. "You afraid I'll join the other side?"

"I tell you, sir," Lix-el addressed his ambassador, "he is trustworthy—completely so. I take full responsibility."

Fas-Ten shrugged. "Very well. We have infiltrated security. We have contacts in the highest circles of government, in business, in communications—"

"I get the picture. This group have a name?"

"The Legion. And it is the Legion which must be my first concern. When I received word of the alert, I came directly here. I prayed that you would contact Ken-Rue immediately, and I could take you all to safety. Coming to this world was a grave error. No one even suspects our existence. But with the true leader of Ardenya here, questions will most certainly be asked. An investigation is sure to follow. It is premature for the Legion to show its hand—"

I interrupted the lecture. "Look, they already know we're here. The cat's out of the bag."

"Not if you moved on," Fas-Ten said excitedly. "The Capital would just be a stopover then. Suspicion would be diverted—"

"Forget that."

"But you must—"

"I mustn't anything. Not since I said bye-bye to the Penal World. That was the whole idea."

"Our safety depends on—"

"Use your head. *"He's* your leader, not me. I'm just an extra in all this. Send *him* on and you can forget about me and the girl."

Fas-Ten opened his mouth, and closed it.

"Think smart," I suggested.

The girl said, "What names did the alert give?"

Fas-Ten looked at her. "Only three. Lix-el, Bar and Ganz. And your descriptions."

"This alert, it was just for the Control World?"

"I assume—"

"You don't know."

"Of course not. How *could* I?"

"Right. Ganz figured there'd be alerts on *all* the worlds, remember? And that's my guess, too. You got carried away, Fas-Ten."

Lix-el spoke up. "I would still be languishing in a cell if it weren't for this man. I, for one, am prepared to put the Legion's resources at his disposal—if he so desires. Besides, he's right. It's me they're after, not him."

Fas-Ten spread his hands, shrugged.

I nodded at Lix-el. "Thanks," I said. To Fas-Ten I said, "The name Van-See mean anything to you?"

He looked startled. "What did you say?"

I told him.

"How did you come by that name?" he asked.

"In a dream."

Lix-el said, "He was a Blank."

"A Blank? He does not *look* like a Blank, let alone *act* like one."

"Thanks for small favors. They bungled the job."

Fas-Ten nodded. "Describe this Van-See."

"He's got very broad shoulders, black lines under his eyes, a habit of rubbing his hands together."

"And you say you have dreamed of him?"

"That's what I said."

"You know such a person?" Lix-el demanded.

The tall ex-ambassador slowly nodded.

"Well, who is he, man? Out with it."

"An adviser to the Chairman."

"I've never heard of him," Lix-el complained.

"He did not crave publicity. It was his nature to remain out of the limelight."

"Was?" Lix-el said. "He is dead?"

"He might as well be," Fas-Ten said.

"What's that supposed to mean?" I asked.

"He's in prison."

"Prison?" I said. "What did he do?"

"Nothing, as far as I know. The Chairman turned against him."

"That's all?"

"It is enough."

The girl said, "Is there no justice?"

"None to speak of," Lix-el said.

"I've got to see him," I said, "this Van-See."

"Insanity," Fas-Ten said. "He is in the dungeon."

"Can't be helped," I said. "If I could get off the Penal World, I can get into a dungeon."

"It is called the dungeon," Fas-Ten said, "because those who enter rarely leave. But it is in every way a modern prison."

"All the better," I said.

"I will accompany you," Lix-el said.

"That is madness," Fas-Ten all but screamed.

"We have no contacts in this dungeon?" Lix-el asked.

"Yes, but if we use them now," Fas-Ten said, "their usefulness to us may be at an end."

"We will chance that, sir," Lix-el said.

I said, "No use sticking your neck in the noose, Lix-el; you've done enough for me."

"He is absolutely right," Fas-Ten said.

"Nonsense. I was imprisoned at the direct behest of the Chairman. I wish a word with this adviser of his. And I am prepared to use the Legion to get it."

— CHAPTER —
Thirty

Block opened his eyes.

"Drink this," Nora said, handing him a glass of water. He took a swallow.

"Thanks."

He looked around. He was lying on a couch in her living room.

"Are you all right, darling?"

"Yes, I think so." He sat up very slowly, like a man whose

bones had turned to cheap plaster, swung his feet onto the floor. "Only I wouldn't bet my last dime on it."

Nora was staring at him. "You're so thin."

"I've kind of been under the weather. You lug me in from the hallway?"

She nodded. She seemed dazed.

"Thanks." He held out his arms.

They clung to each other a good long time. Her cheek, he noted, was smooth, warm and fit perfectly next to his.

"Sweetheart, what happened to you?"

There it was, the question he'd been waiting for, the very same one he'd been asking himself. Only now, maybe, he had a few answers.

Nora sat next to him. They held hands. Sunlight shone through the windows. The sound of traffic and kids yelling came from the street below. He felt the tension draining out of him.

"How long have I been gone, honey?"

"Almost nine months."

"Uh-huh, sounds about right."

"Why didn't you call or write, sweetie? Why didn't you tell me — tell someone — you were going away? *Why?"*

"I didn't know I *was* going away, that's why."

"What was it, something you *had* to keep secret?"

He shook his head. "Nothing like that."

"Then what?"

"Would you believe I spent the last nine months just a few blocks from here?"

"Were you . . . *hiding* from someone?"

"Maybe from myself."

"I don't *understand,* darling."

"I was a bum, Nora, a deadbeat. I hung out on skid row and got loaded on cheap whiskey."

"Ross . . . "

"It's true, every word of it; Scout's honor."

"You *must* be joking. A derelict?"

"Yeah. Plain and simple. I spent more time in the gutter than in the flophouses. Half the time I was so stewed I didn't know where I was or who I was. I got to know the Men's Shelter inside out." The two words seemed to echo through his mind. *Men's Shelter. Men's Shelter.* Something important about the Men's Shelter. What was it? "I lived on nickels and dimes," Block said, "and the clothes on my back looked like something the cleaning man kept around to use on toilets."

Nora's hand had grown cold in his. "But if you were in some kind of trouble, you could've always come to me, to Ben Cohen, to the paper."

"Sure, if I'd remembered any of you."

"What are you saying?"

"I had so many holes in my memory, I didn't know which side was up. You, my friends, most of my recent past, it was all a big blank."

"You had *amnesia?*"

"Yes, something like that. Probably I just drank myself into such a stupor that I simply blacked out."

"But *why?*"

"Because two old friends of mine died, and I stood by and did nothing. Worse, I ran away and hid. Can you beat that? It's all come back to me. I remember now. Listen, I'd been having this nightmare, see? I shoot someone. And a flat-nosed guy shoots me. Only it never happened! Guilt, that's what it was. My unconscious made up a lot of shit to *repress* the real story: *how I let my friends die.* And the flat-nosed guy somehow must be in with the killers. I'd been dreaming about him. But I had him in the wrong setting, that's all. This was the Nash thing, honey. Pavel and Anna knew Nash, and they were going to help me."

The story came pouring out of him, like water flooding over a dam. The ride with Pavel and Anna. The house in the country. The three goons who crawled out of the woodwork. The shootout. And what he'd done. "That's the worst of it. Maybe I could've saved them. If I hadn't gone off to the basement, they might've had a chance. They were my friends and I let them down. It's just as though I'd pulled the trigger. *The blame's mine! I've got to accept that.*"

Nora was looking at him, her face tight. "What is it?" he asked.

"Honey, what did you do afterward, when you drove back to the city?"

"Afterward?" He shrugged. "Probably busy getting blotto. I had plenty of reason."

"But you're not sure?"

"Uh-uh."

"Do you remember *anything* from that time?"

"It's real hazy."

"And you've been drinking steadily since then?"

"Just about."

Nora shook her head. "It's all wrong!"

"What is?"

"Your story, darling. It doesn't make sense."

"It makes sense to me."

"Does it?"

"Sure."

"Ross, you don't drink the hard stuff; just white wine."

I shrugged. "Didn't maybe."

"No, sweetie, you've never drunk. You don't like the taste, don't like what it does to you."

"There's always a first time."

"Alcohol makes you *sick*. Don't you remember that?"

"Maybe I just didn't care this time."

"Because you felt responsible for what happened to those two people?"

"Because I felt responsible."

"This Anna and professor you were so broken up over, they were friends of yours? Old, close friends?"

I nodded. "That's why it hit me so hard, I guess."

"Darling, how long have we known each other?"

"Us? About eight years."

"Were we close? Real close?"

"You don't have to ask."

"Anna, the professor, you saw them often?"

"Sure."

"You did things together?"

"Uh-huh."

"And they met your other friends, of course?"

"That's right."

"What's the professor's first name?"

He shrugged. "My head's still woozy, I guess."

"Honey, for you to go bonkers like this, those two would have had to be very important people in your life. Like a sister or brother, almost. *Ross, I never even heard of them!*"

"Nora . . ."

"Why would you keep them a secret from me? *And how?* We were together so often. And if they were old friends, what were they doing with Marty Nash? Why didn't you go

169

to them right off the bat when you started looking for Nash?"

He could feel the sweat breaking out on his forehead. Something echoed in his mind: *Men's Shelter, Men's Shelter.* He was going to be sick.

"I went to the police, sweetheart. So did Ben Cohen. You were a missing person. And they looked for you. Maybe you were on the Bowery this month, or last. But not nine months ago. Not back then. They looked for you and they couldn't find you."

The room had started going round. *Men's Shelter* rang in his mind like a scream. He heard Nora's voice coming from a vast distance.

"You didn't crack up because of those two. And you didn't go on a nine-month drunk. Someone did something to you, honey. Someone or something set you up."

— CHAPTER —

Thirty-One

The dungeon was high up on a hill in the northwest section of town.

The first rays of the rising sun fell across the city streets as we rode through the prison's high gates in the bread wagon. The odor of fresh-baked bread drifted around us.

I glanced into the rear-view mirror. The heavy metal gates were swinging shut behind us. My stomach did a flip-flop. It was too soon to be back behind prison walls. I could feel the sweat breaking out on my forehead. If I didn't watch out, I'd give the whole game away.

Lix-el sat stolidly by my side. If he was worried in any way, he didn't show it.

We were both dressed in brown uniforms, wore brown caps with visors—the get-up of the Excelsior Bread

Company. The man at the wheel wore the uniform, too. Of the three of us, he was the only one entitled to it.

We pulled up at a back door.

Two guards and three maties were waiting for us. The maties began to unload the bread. Our driver stayed with them. Lix-el and I walked into the kitchen. Maties were at work at the five giant stoves, at the tables, in the storage rooms, the freezer.

We didn't bother them. We kept going.

Assistant Warden Flack held down the last office in a long gray corridor. He was a thin, worried-looking man in his early fifties, seated behind a small desk. This Flack was a low-level warden, working the night shift; he was a member of the Legion.

His eyes boggled when he saw Lix-el.

"I had no idea—" he said in a small, reedy voice.

Lix-el nodded, smiled, extended a hand and said, "Now you know how important this is."

Flack seemed stunned. "But the risk, sir . . ." His voice petered out.

"We'll be gone before you know it," Lix-el said cheerily. "Are those the clothes?"

Flack wagged his head. Two black Warder uniforms, third-class, rested on a folding chair. We peeled off our baker outfits, climbed into Warder garb. We didn't waste any time doing it.

Flack raised a finger, bit it, pointed it at us. "You have less than an hour. I go off duty at eight. My replacement is not one of us."

For that matter, I wasn't one of us either. I let it ride.

Lix-el told him not to worry.

Flack said, "I will personally escort you to the cell. Here is a special pass. Unnecessary, I'm sure, but merely in case. For God's sake, keep track of the time."

We followed Flack up the gray corridor. The Warder uniform didn't cheer me at all; it wasn't even a good fit. We took the speed-lift up three levels. Here the walls were gray too, but the gray of solid metal.

Flack stopped before a cell, applied the code clip to the receptor.

Metal door slid open. Lights snapped on in the cell. A

171

man sat up on his bunk. His shoulders were wide, his black hair streaked with white. His nose resembled a beak. Dark lines were under his eyes.

I took a step forward.

Van-See saw me. And fainted dead away!

Flack had left.

Van-See sat on his cot, stared at us.

Cell lights still ran at nocturnal half-mast. Van-See's eyes were very bright.

"Yes, I know you, my dear boy; if not I, then who? But how did you come to seek me out?"

"I kept seeing you in a dream."

"A dream, you say?"

"Yeah. You and a small fat man. And some party with a flat nose. Mean anything?"

"Amazing."

"No doubt," Lix-el said, "but what does it mean, sir?"

Van-See said, "You are who?"

"Lix-el. Formerly of Ardenya."

"Ah," Van-See said.

"You know him?" I asked.

"He was Prime Minister. The Chairman had him deposed."

"And imprisoned," Lix-el added.

"Of course. The two go together."

"I hardly deserved such treatment," Lix-el said. "Why was I singled out?"

"Because, my dear man, you were a known ally of Pabst."

"Pabst?" I said.

Van-See smiled. "The party with the flat nose."

Lix-el said, "I was his friend—one of many, I should think —not his ally."

"In the Chairman's eyes, that was the *very* same thing."

I asked, "Who was this Pabst?"

"The Chairman's chief adviser," Lix-el said. "Why would my friendship with Pabst disturb the Chairman? It is senseless."

"Oh dear, no," Van-See said. "It makes perfect sense. The Chairman feared that Pabst would overthrow him."

Lix-el glowered at the seated figure. "Poppycock."

"Ah, but you are wrong, my dear man. That was indeed Pabst's intention."

"You know this for a fact?" Lix-el demanded.

"It *is* a fact. The Chairman *was* overthrown. And Pabst has taken his place."

"Surely Fas-Ten would have told me," Lix-el said.

"If he *knew*," Van-See pointed out.

"It just happened?" I asked.

"Oh, no, my dear boy—almost a full year now."

"How have they kept this a secret, then?" Lix-el asked.

"A double has taken the Chairman's place."

"And the Chairman?"

"Dead."

Lix-el was silent.

"Let me guess," I said. "The Chairman is a small fat man."

"With blond hair," Van-See said. "That *was* the Chairman."

"Great," I said. "I've been dreaming about public officials. And here I thought I had an inside track."

"Ah, but you do, my dear boy."

"Maybe you'd like to tell me?"

"Of course I shall. You were the Chairman's captain of the guards."

"I was?"

"And a very good one, at that."

"I had a name?"

"Amtroy."

I shrugged.

Van-See beamed. "You cannot expect to remember, my dear boy. You were erased."

"Why?"

"There was a coup. The fracas was quite terrible. As captain, you led the loyal guards in defense of the Chairman. You were most heroic. But it was all to no avail. The Chairman was killed, you captured, and I, ultimately, imprisoned."

I looked at him. "That's it?"

Van-See nodded. "In a nutshell," he said, and rubbed his hands together. I remembered that little trick. From my dream.

"Could be," I said. "I remember you, okay. I remember Pabst. I even remember the Chairman. *But not me.* How come?"

Van-See sighed. "It could not be helped."

"You sound as though it were your fault," I said.

Van-See spread his hands. "In part."

"Let's hear it," I said.

"Are XI tapes familiar to you?"

"No."

"They will be. When your memory continues to improve. XI tapes have been a closely guarded secret."

"I know about X tapes," I told him.

"Ah."

"They run the Blanks. I used to be one of them before I began to remember."

"That, my dear boy, was the XI tape remembering, not you."

Lix-el glanced at me questioningly. I shrugged a shoulder. "Better explain that," I said.

"XI tapes contain a person's memories *and* personality. An astounding breakthrough, wouldn't you say?"

"And I've got one of these XI tapes?"

"Yes. You were exposed to one."

"Then I should get it all back, remember who I am and what I did, right?"

"I'm afraid not, my dear boy. You were not fed your own memories, but someone else's."

"*Whose?*"

"The Chairman's."

I plunked down on the cot. It was either that or fall over.

"You mean," I heard myself say, "I'm going to become the Chairman?"

"In time, yes. You will have his memories. And personality. It is unavoidable."

"But *why?*" I whispered. "How did this thing happen?"

"It was my doing," Van-See said, "but I had no choice. The Chairman was dying; he had sustained a mortal wound. But I had managed to drag him to the transfer room. It is in his residence, on a lower floor."

"A small white-walled room," I said.

"Yes. I collected the Chairman's memories seconds before he passed on. I recorded them on the reverse side of an X tape. An electric charge had rendered you and the other guards unconscious, my dear boy. I found you in the Great Hall. An X tape had already been tagged to your sleeve; you were to be carried off and processed within the hour. I substituted the Chairman's tape. To all appearances, it was an unused X tape. But I knew the reverse side would filter through, when administered, and ultimately the Chairman's memory and personality would come to the fore. As they have. Your memory is, alas, gone forever. But the Chairman's will live!"

"Thanks loads."

"Think nothing of it, my dear boy. It was the least I could do. You still have your noble body. The Chairman will like that."

"And *I'm* the Chairman."

"You are indeed."

"I don't like it."

"You will learn to. When more of his memories become yours."

"I can hardly wait."

"It may take time, of course."

"How much time?"

"My dear boy, who can say? Using the reverse side of an X tape to store and transmit XI data is a true innovation. It has, to the best of my knowledge, never been done before. Your case will tell us much of how it works."

"My case."

Lix-el said, "How many know the Chairman is this man?"

"Only I. And now you two."

"I'm sorry I asked," I said.

Lix-el turned to me. "If he is right, you will shortly become the Chairman."

"Don't remind me."

Van-See beamed. "You will have at your fingertips, my dear boy, the greatest secrets of state—not to mention science. Isn't that wonderful?"

"Yeah, just dandy."

"Your life won't be worth much," Lix-el told me, "if Pabst finds out."

"I thought he was your pal," I said.

"He kept me in prison. I am better off casting my lot with you."

"Me."

"The true Chairman," Van-See said, rubbing his hands together.

Lix-el said, "We have helped each other. We both feel that freedom has suffered."

"Along with us," I said.

"And you, sir, won't send me back to a cell, will you?" Lix-el said.

"Cut it out."

Van-See said, "You will regain your rightful seat, my dear boy, as soon as your mind is firm again."

"It's firm enough now," I said.

"You understand," Lix-el said, "that we cannot leave him here."

"Of course not, my dear friends; we are as one now."

"It's going to be a mess," I said. "Getting him out will sink Flack and turn this whole town on its ear. It might even tip them that we've landed."

"It can't be helped," Lix-el said.

I sighed. "I suppose not."

Flack's face drained of color when the three of us marched into his office.

We'd kept Van-See between us on our trek through the corridors, down the speed-lift and over to Flack. No one had stopped us. But we'd gotten more than our share of attention. The dungeon was waking up, activity starting to crowd the hallways. Getting Van-See out was going to be a problem.

"What *have* you done?" Flack shrieked, jumping to his feet. "Get him back to his cell! *At once!*"

"Flack!" Lix-el said sternly. "Control yourself."

Flack didn't even hear him. "Are you *mad?*" he babbled. "He's our most *important* prisoner. You were just supposed to talk to him, not take him for a walk. If word gets out, I'll lose my job. Quick, take him back!"

"You don't understand, Flack," Lix-el said. "He must come with us."

"He must *what?*"

"He has knowledge," Lix-el said, "which is of grave importance to the Legion, which could change the course of history. We are at a turning point, sir. The Chairman and his corrupt regime are about to fall. It would be best if you came with us, too."

"Come with you?" Flack sputtered.

"It will not be safe here," Lix-el said, "after we have gone."

"*Safe?* I'll be shot!"

"Oh dear yes," Van-See said, rubbing his hands together. "They will be merciless."

"Precisely," Lix-el said. "It is for your own good, sir."

"Good?" Flack yelled. "You're *crazy*. Yes, I joined the Legion. But not to end up in front of a firing squad! You expect me to become a fugitive, turn my back on everything I've worked for, at the mere drop of a hat?"

Lix-el said, "It is not a request, sir. It is an order."

"Order? Who are you to give me orders? I am warden here, not you!"

Flack's hand moved toward a button on his desk.

"Don't do that," I said. I held a long-nosed blaster in my hand, its muzzle pointed at Flack.

"You dare threaten me *here?*" Flack all but screamed.

"I'll do more than threaten," I growled, "if you don't behave yourself."

"Have you lost your reason?"

"We'll argue later," I told him. "Right now we're getting out of here. And you're joining us."

"I am not!"

"You want to die?" I asked simply.

Van-See said, "A firing squad, my dear friend, is mere conjecture. But if you fail to cooperate now, your death in the next few minutes is an absolute certainty."

"That's the way it is, Flack," I said. "What's your choice?"

Five of us left the prison by way of the kitchen. Three were dressed in the brown uniforms of the baking company. The other pair wore civilian clothing. The papers handed the guards at the gate identified two kitchen workers on the night shift. It wasn't the first time, Flack had told us, that prison personnel had hitched a ride with a delivery van. But it would probably be the last.

Lix-el drove. I began to peel off my uniform. It was tough going in the small cabin.

"Put our guests under wrap," I told Lix-el. "And let me off at the next corner. I've got some business to attend to."

"But you *can't*," Lix-el said. "It's far too dangerous."

I shrugged. "What isn't these days?"

— CHAPTER —
Thirty-Two

Ross Block walked along the Bowery. He felt weak and hollow, as if his insides had been sucked out and only a brittle shell remained.

The tattered buildings called to him like old friends. Doorways urged him to rest his feet, grab a wink. Liquor stores beckoned, promised high times out of a bottle.

Dirt-encrusted derelicts sat on the sidewalks, in doorways, dragged themselves along the street, their hair matted, cheeks sunken, clothes soiled and shredded.

A short, toothless bum tottered over to him, murmured, "Can you help me out, mister?"

Block fumbled in his pocket, came up with some loose change, tossed it into the man's hand, shuddered and hurried on. He'd been one of them once, maybe still was; he didn't know. . . .

He seemed to see everything in triple vision, as though three brains were lodged in his skull: the bum, the reporter and someone else. None of the brains appeared too bright.

Then he was standing in front of the Men's Shelter, looking up at the weathered four-story structure. The building seemed to pull at him, the houses, parked cars, streetlamps whirled around his head. Sounds flowed together, rang in his ears. He was moving on legs which belonged to a stranger.

The little man was there, as usual, in the Big Room

among the empty chairs, the stench of Lysol and sweat. He was bald, skinny, dressed in a black T-shirt with the word "sexy" emblazoned on it.

"Hello, Knobby."

The floor sweep looked at him.

"What can I do for you?" he asked.

Block had his trenchcoat on, wore neat clothes, a tie, jacket, was clean-shaven: Some difference.

"It's me, Knobby, Ross Block."

The floor sweep's eyes became very round. "Mr. Block?"

"Uh-huh." Block grinned, held out his hand. The shorter man took it hesitantly, shook it.

"What happened, Mr. Block? You make good?"

The whirlwind around Block had died as suddenly as it had begun. The worn floorboards felt solid under his feet. He nodded.

"Something like that."

"You go on the wagon, Mr. Block?"

"Yes."

"You chuck it cold-turkey?"

"Uh-huh, just about."

"I hardly recognized you, Mr. Block. Still can't get over it."

"I remembered who I was, what I was."

"But it's only been a day."

"Quick recovery." Block grinned.

"I'm glad, Mr. Block, real glad for you. Don't often see a man pull himself together like that. Not down here. Almost never."

"I know. I remember all you did for me, Knobby."

"Don't mention it, Mr. Block."

Block held a fifty-dollar bill in his hand. "For you, Knobby. It's not enough, but—"

"You're mistaken, Mr. Block; it's too much, way too much. I loaned you less than five."

"Take it," Block said. "Please."

He stuck it into the floor sweep's pocket.

The little man seemed stunned. "It really isn't necessary, Mr. Block."

"It is—for me."

"It's a miracle, Mr. Block. You being well again. I can't get over it, I just can't."

Knobby shook Block's hand again; he was grinning from ear to ear.

"Knobby," Block said, "I left something with you, didn't I?"

"Sure thing, Mr. Block, I haven't forgotten." He broke into another smile. "The collateral," he said. "For the loan. Wasn't more than four dollars. Didn't want any collateral. But you insisted, said you wanted me to keep it."

"Smartest thing I ever did. You still have what I gave you?"

"What do you think, course I do. Just follow me, Mr. Block."

They left the Big Room, went into a short corridor, down a flight of wooden stairs, into the basement.

Light came from a single naked light bulb.

The floor sweep went to a battered locker, fished a key from his pocket, opened it, reached inside.

In his hands he held a package, a brown paper bag tied with cord.

He gave it to Block.

Not very heavy, Block thought. He said, "Would you mind leaving me alone with this, Knobby? There's something I've got to see."

"You bet, Mr. Block; of course. I didn't touch it. It's just the way you gave it to me."

"I know that, Knobby. What's in here is kind of personal, that's all."

The floor sweep waved a half salute, went back up the stairs.

Block was alone.

He stared at his package.

For all he knew the only items it contained were some old socks and underwear. Or maybe a bottle of cheap booze. No telling what an alkie might squirrel away.

The flickers were obviously the symptoms of a deranged mind. And now that he had his wits about him, the thing to do was check into the nearest funny farm.

Only the guys from the flickers had turned up in real life, had stepped out of his boozed-up dreams and were chasing after him and each other with drawn guns.

That changed things.

Maybe he *had* shot someone. Maybe this Professor Pavel

and Anna *had* tried to blow the whistle on McCoy Imports and gotten gunned down for their trouble.

It was possible, all right.

Maybe he'd tangled with Marty Nash's killers and come out on the short end of the stick. Maybe they'd given him something — a drug of some sort — that had scrambled his brains, turned him into a rummy, made him forget who he was.

Sure.

But why hadn't they knocked him off outright, left him in some dark alley to rot? Wouldn't that have been a lot smoother?

He didn't know.

He remembered who he was now; the bits and pieces of his life finally fit together. He remembered identifying Nash, hunting around his old Brooklyn neighborhood, getting the green light from Ben Cohen, and deciding to visit Charles Hastings at McCoy. But that was where everything stopped cold. The rest was a hodgepodge, a madman's nightmare, with unfamiliar leering faces, guns going off, bodies falling, hands reaching for him.

The rest was the important part, and it made no sense to him.

Nora was right: he'd been set up. And until he found out why, he was the pigeon in the soup.

The cord holding the package together was tied into small knots. He had no knife. It took a while to untie them.

Block ripped open the paper bag.

A small, rectangular box lay in his hand.

He recognized it all right.

It was the one from the flickers.

"Block!" The voice was hard, monotone.

Ross Block looked up.

There were two of them by the stairs, two of his nightmare creations, the pair that had popped out of his dreams — to kill him. *And they were together.*

The redhead with the jutting chin and green parka leaned against the wall, his hands stuck in his pockets, a huge grin on his face.

"Hi, palsy," he said. "See you found it, huh?"

The thin, flat-nosed man wasn't smiling. "Led us a merry chase, Block," he said.

He held a gun in his hand, the one with the silencer. It was pointed squarely at Block.

Block's eyes hunted for a way out, someplace to run to hide. There was none. He was stuck inside these four walls. Only a bench and locker here. And his one exit, the staircase, was blocked.

The strength drained from him like liquid from a cracked bottle. He felt old, used up, as fragile as a cracked eggshell. The small box was suddenly very heavy in his grip.

"How did you find me?" he heard himself say.

"Easy, palsy. Look in your right coat pocket."

Block looked.

At first his fingers found nothing. Then he touched something small, circular.

He pulled it out.

The object in Block's palm could have been a tiny watch, but wasn't. He had never seen anything like it before.

"Homing device, palsy; tagged you while you was sleepin'. We been sittin' on your tail all day. Coulda been worse. You remembered real quick."

"Almost tagged you myself, Block. In the flophouse. But you woke up too soon. Caused us a good deal of trouble."

Block said, "I thought you'd come to kill me."

"Premature," the flat-nosed man said. "Not then."

"You shot at me."

"Necessary. To pressure you, Block, to stir your mind to wakefulness."

"The box, palsy; we had to make you remember where you stashed it. Best way was to squeeze you, put the screws on tight."

Block said, "You two were together from the start."

"Yeah."

"You weren't shooting at each other."

"We were stringin' you, palsy."

The flat-nosed man sighed. "Exposed yourself to an XI tape, Block. Altered your mind. Dimmed out your memory. Only temporary. The mind revives under pressure."

Block said, "Pavel, his daughter—that was all real."

"Sure, palsy, whaddya think? We trailed you from McCoy. You and the Pavels led us to where Nash buried the box. Only you grabbed it and gave us the slip."

"Began to remember, Block; the pressure brought it

out. Would have remembered more in time—too much."

Block said, "I shot someone, a short fat man with blond hair, and you stepped out of the crowd—"

"And shot you?"

"Yes. That was . . . real too?"

"Real, Block. Never happened to you. Someone else's memory—in your brain now."

"I . . . I don't get it."

"Too soon, Block. Later it would come back, all of it. Know everything. Can't let that happen."

"Yeah, palsy, too bad for you."

The redhead had a gun too.

"Wait," Block said desperately. "Listen. You can have the box. Take anything you want. All this is crazy. It's got to be a gag. *Someone else's memory—?*"

"Sorry, palsy, tough break."

"Box is ours, Block, what we needed to move ahead. Can't let you jeopardize everything."

Block heard the hammer click on the redhead's gun.

"Bye, palsy."

"No! Please!"

Block remembered what had happened the last time he'd opened the box. But was the memory true?

His fingers flipped back the twin lids.

White light pierced his eyeballs, stabbed through his mind.

It felt as if a sledge hammer had struck his head. His skull seemed to explode.

Then there was nothing.

— CHAPTER —
Thirty-Three

It looked every bit a palace.

Nine levels tall. A quarter link wide. With domes and towers aplenty rising out of the roof.

The Chairman's residence, glittering gold and silver in

the morning sun. I let my eyes take it all in from the safety of a distant corner.

Not half bad.

And I was the Chairman.

I grinned to myself. I had to watch out, not let my new status go to my head. Only three people in the whole universe knew who I really was. And none of us looked too trustworthy.

Possibly with a little luck, I'd turn out not to be the Chairman, after all. I'd like that.

There were sentries at all the doors, and a metal fence wound its way around the edifice.

No way to walk in without an appointment.

I didn't let it bother me.

I turned on my heel, went away from there. I didn't go very far.

A two-level house stood on the next corner. I went to its door, pressed my finger against the indent.

A man presently opened the door—medium height, broad shoulders, on the youngish side.

"Yes?"

"Two kings are better than one," I said.

He gazed at me blankly. "What?"

The code phrase was a bit dated. By as much as a year, I was willing to bet. Nuts.

I slugged him.

He was tougher than I'd figured.

He bounced off the wall, cuffed me with a right.

A doorstep brawl was the last thing I needed.

I put my fist in his belly, doubling him over; I chopped him on the neck, brought my knee up into his face.

I didn't have to hit him again; he was done.

I dragged him inside, shoved the door closed with a foot, left him on the floor and hurried off toward the rear of the house.

I didn't think this lad was alone here; I wanted to be gone by the time company showed up.

The fourth room I entered was my baby. The mind-flow was going strong now, the clicks pouring in on me.

I pressed part of the wall, and watched it slide open.

I stepped through.

The wall slid back into place.

Dust was everywhere.

It suddenly occurred to me that I might've beaten up an innocent bystander. With the big shots on ice, no one would know about this room.

The transmitter was by the wall. I turned on the juice, dialed the right co-ords, stepped on the platform and was whisked away.

I felt nothing.

One instant I was in the back room, the next in the Chairman's house.

I stepped off the platform.

I was in a small, gray-ceilinged chamber. There was dust here too, a sure sign of disuse. I grinned. All this was old hat to me.

Seeing the towers through the window had sprung my memory.

I knew now that I could remember in three different ways:

Under pressure.

In the course of time.

Or by seeing some key sight.

Simple.

Except the course of time would take years. And the pressure could kill you. And there might not be any key sights handy if you were off on a prison world.

The last thing you did returned first, could play itself over and over again in your mind till you hit the next item.

The last thing could become a nightmare, a replay that would go on endlessly.

The towers had done the trick. And hearing Van-See's story about the XI tapes had made another piece shift into place.

I still didn't know who I was.

I had only part of the picture.

But I knew how the memory tapes worked.

And I knew where they were kept.

The mansion was honeycombed with hidden passageways. I used one now. I wondered how much the phony Chairman had going for him, whether he really ran the show or was just a stooge.

Stooge was more likely.

The transmitter was too much of a good thing to put in mothballs.

As I marched, I gave my hallway the once-over.

Dim glowers burned overhead, some were dark. The place smelled moldy. I could hear no sounds. All this privacy cheered me. I wanted to go about my work undisturbed.

An electro-eye winked at me, another wall slid open, and I was inside the tape bank.

I recognized it, all right.

The white walls, table, and the skullcap device.

I'd seen the small blond man stretched out on this table. The notion that he was me wasn't very pleasant.

I went to the opposite wall; it slid back, revealing two shelves. Only some sixty tape cartridges there. This XI tape business, according to Van-See, was still in its experimental stage, hadn't really gotten off the ground.

My name, Van-See had said, was Amtroy.

The cartridges were labeled.

One bore the name Amtroy.

I took a deep breath. Van-See didn't know it all. Someone had been nice enough to collect what was left of me in this cartridge. I wasn't a lost cause after all.

I slipped the tape into its playback slit, put on the skullcap, stretched out on the table, gripped the on switch.

Just like old times—for the Chairman.

The Chairman had fed himself plenty of tapes, all of the sixty probably. A couple were labeled with people's names But most were learning tapes.

The Chairman hadn't bothered with jumpers and space ships, wasn't planning a jaunt through the universe.

So I hadn't known how to pilot those vessels.

The Chairman flew a hovercraft. So I could, too.

The Chairman had no interest in working a computer Which was why the skill wasn't kicking around in my head and I had to use the girl.

But who could complain?

The Chairman was a walking encyclopedia. The bits of knowledge I'd been able to unscramble in my brain had saved my skin.

And now, possibly, I'd get the lowdown on the real me.

I flipped the switch.

White light flooded my mind. I heard myself scream. My brain seemed to smash open.

I sailed off into a white, shimmering haze.

I drifted back to consciousness slowly, painfully.

I didn't know how much time had gone by.

My noggin felt as if someone had been using it for target practice. I realized now I might've jumped the gun in fooling with these XI tapes. The process seemed still to have a few kinks in it.

Rolling off the table, I got to my feet. At least I could stand up.

I fished through my mind hunting for a trace of Amtroy. And found him.

Amtroy had been a gladiator, had fought in some of the swankiest rinks on the Control World. He'd won most of his bouts, become a somebody and started to hobnob with the Arm bigshots. When he got too old to bust skulls his new pals found him a better job — as one of the Chairman's bodyguards.

There were only a couple of catches to my being this Amtroy.

He was a big, ugly bruiser, almost the size, if not the width, of Bar.

And he'd been dead at least a decade.

Van-See had got it all wrong.

I grinned sourly.

Time for another chat with the Chairman's ex-adviser; he might prove even more enlightening than these tapes. I didn't want to monkey with any more XIs, in any case, till I figured out what I was doing wrong.

I left the white-walled room.

I didn't go back to the transmitter chamber. Tangling with whoever might be in the corner house didn't appeal to me. I hadn't sifted through Amtroy's memories; they were still sketchy in my mind. But the gladiator turned bodyguard had known a thing or two. And one of those things was an emergency way out of this place. It would mean popping up for an instant in the mansion proper. But once I hit the other passage, it'd be clear sailing. A ten-minute stroll underground and I'd come up in a different section of the city.

The door slid open at the right place. I stepped out onto a thick rug. A quick glance to the right and left showed me the corridor was deserted. I could hear sounds now, but nothing close by.

The passage I wanted was in the Chairman's bedroom. An escape route in case of trouble, built into the place long before the transmitter had turned up.

I moved fast, was at the door in no time. I had my hand on the knob when I heard the voice.

It was deep, husky, and came from inside the room.

It was the voice of the blond-haired girl.

— CHAPTER —
Thirty-Four

Block opened his eyes.

He was flat on his back in the basement of the Men's Shelter.

He wasn't alone.

The flat-nosed guy and his pal, the redhead, were stretched out by the stairs. Both were sleeping peacefully.

White light filled the cellar, blazed against the wall, bounced off the ceiling.

The light came from the small double-lidded box on the floor next to Block. He could look at it now with no ill effects. Two spheres nestled in the box, a partition separating them. Each lid fit over one of the spheres.

Block sighed, closed both lids.

Only one naked lightbulb burned. The rest of the cellar was covered by shadows.

He felt the back of his head where he'd landed on the concrete. Just sore, not bleeding.

Ross Block sat quietly on the floor.

After a while he rose, picked up the box, put it in his coat pocket, and went up the stairs.

"Everything all right, Mr. Block?" Knobby said.

"For a while, no. It is now."

"What do you mean?"

"Had some visitors down there. Two guys with guns."

"You're joking?"

"Uh-uh."

"What happened, Mr. Block?"

"I laid them out."

The floor sweep stared at him.

"They're sleeping like babies. Better call the cops."

"Mr. Block, do I mention you?"

He shrugged. "If you want."

"What do I say?"

"They've got guns, Knobby. Doesn't matter what you say. The cops'll be interested."

"If you say so, Mr. Block."

"Thanks again, Knobby, for everything. I'll be around."

Block went out into the street. The sun was almost overhead—high noon.

He turned, walked away from the Bowery.

The taxi let him off on the highway.

He paid the driver, started up the gravel road.

Overhead, the sky was a clear blue. Green fields stretched off into the distance.

The path curved through a wooded area. A shallow stream paralleled it for a few yards, then curved away. He heard birds, smelled lush vegetation.

The house he came to was a three-story job of wood and shingles, unpainted and weathered to a dull gray.

The windows were shuttered, the door locked.

Block went to work on a shutter.

After a while, he got it open.

He crawled through the window, looked back once at the countryside, turned and disappeared into the house.

— CHAPTER —
Thirty-Five

I eased open the door.

The short, yellow-haired lad with the potbelly and thick lips was up against the wall. He had on a purple dressing gown. He was sweating plenty, but not because he was overdressed; he had better, more urgent reasons.

The blond girl was busy pointing a long-nosed laser his way. Her lips were two tight lines in a white, drawn face.

Behind her, part of the wall was slid back, revealing a dark passageway—the one I'd been going to use.

"I am guiltless . . . guiltless!" the phony Chairman shrieked.

"You are a *murderer,*" the girl hissed.

"Not I! The others perhaps; it is they—"

"You are scum!" the girl said.

She squeezed the trigger.

A needle beam blazed from the laser, sliced into the small man. He screamed once, his flailing hands trying to ward off the charge. He crumpled to the floor. The odor of scorched flesh drifted toward me.

I stood there with my mouth hanging open, my eyes boggling out of my head. Stupefied was too mild a word to describe my condition.

"Why did you do that?" I heard myself say in a voice I hardly recognized.

Her green eyes turned toward me.

"Ah, the other assassin."

I almost looked behind me to see who she was addressing.

The laser was firm in her hand. It was aimed at me.

"Step in," she ordered.

I stepped in.

"Listen," I said, "I don't know what you're—"

"Silence!"

I shut up.

The girl drew herself up to her full height, glared at me.

"Know me for who I am," she said. "I am Adinah, the Chairman's daughter!"

"No kidding?" I said. "That's swell, but—"

"He died here in this house."

"Who?"

"My father."

"I know."

"Cut down, as he stood with his friends."

"I'm sorry."

"And I, I was taken unconscious to the erasure chamber. They made me forget. But I remember now. *And I remember you.*"

"Look—" I said.

"Assassin!"

"Wait a second."

"Killer!"

"Lady, hold it. I'm the boy who saved your hide, who got you off the Penal World."

"Swine! I will do to you what you did to my father."

"You've got it wrong. Use your head; if I'd killed the Chairman, if I were in on the plot, what was I doing on the Penal World? I should've been sitting pretty here in the Capital, not rotting on a digger. Someone's been feeding you a line, trying to divide us. Don't let 'em. Whoever gave you this junk is on the other side."

"Liar!"

"Who was it? Fas-Ten? Ken-Rue, Flack? *Who got to you?*"

"No one!"

"Don't hand me that. *Someone's* been ribbing you. I want his name. You've got to give me a chance to clear myself, to come up with some answers. You owe me that much."

"You have no chance, murderer! No one spoke to me, no one uttered a word against you. It is *I* who remember, *I* who call you killer."

"Remember, huh?"

Her green eyes seemed on fire. "Yes!"

"How?"

"The white sphere."

"The what?"

"The XI tapes."

"You know about that?"

191

"I am Adinah, the Chairman's daughter. I know all."

"I think I liked you better the other way."

"Silence, dog! You dare mock me?"

"I wasn't riding you, lady, just stating a fact. What about the XIs?"

"The white spheres *are* portable XIs. They can be administered anywhere."

"And you were fed one?"

"Fool! I was given my true identity."

"How? By whom?"

"Van-See."

"I just freed him."

"That was eight hours ago."

"I was out seven hours?"

"What is it you have done—used the tape bank?"

"Yeah."

"The tape must be properly adjusted, dog, or it will render you senseless."

"It did."

"Then you know the instrument of your undoing. For the tape has delayed you here until my arrival. And now you will die."

"We had a deal, lady. Don't get carried away. You were going to tell me about the XIs, how you pegged me for the killing."

"There is nothing to tell. Before the agents of Pabst could drag me off, Van-See collected my memories in a white sphere, hid it here in the mansion. Then he too was felled. After you freed him he was brought to Ken-Rue's home. He recognized me, gave me instructions on how to enter the mansion, retrieve the sphere. I did as he advised. He is a noble and courageous man, my father's true friend, and he has suffered much for that friendship."

"Yeah. You used this passageway, got in here."

"The impostor slept. He heard nothing."

"You crept out of the room, found the sphere, and used it."

She nodded.

"It put you under?"

"I too was rendered senseless. But for a shorter period, for Van-See had instructed me. I woke. And knew myself for Adinah."

"Great. Tell me something."

"What, pig?"

"How did you know these memories are really yours, belong in your mind?"

"Idiot! My image of myself and what I see in the mirror are identical!"

"Okay. That makes you Adinah. Congratulations. You wanted your memory back and now you've got it. But your thinking I killed the Chairman is way off. Listen, your pal, Van-See, was an eyewitness, saw the whole thing while you were passed out. He said I went to bat for your father, put my life on the line trying to save him."

The gun quivered in her hand. "Van-See lied so you would aid in his escape. I too was an eyewitness, was subdued only after my father's murder. I also saw the whole thing. *You are the murderer.*"

I said, "Give me a second, will you, to think this over."

"A second is all you will have."

"Thanks."

I put the dream back in my mind, gave it a replay.

The Chairman was there, surrounded by his cronies. I saw the gathering was some kind of party. People were laughing, drinking, taking long drags of dream powder. I recognized some of them now. I caught sight of Pabst in the crowd. Van-See was on the other side of the room. The blonde, Adinah, was there too. It was all coming together. I seemed to have double vision, was seeing the room from two angles. I wondered if this accounted for the haze.

A figured moved near the door; he was a blur of motion.

I adjusted my sights, tried to focus on the figure.

Instead, the Chairman was before my eyes. His face white, lips parted; he was backing up, his hand half raised as if trying to ward off a blow.

I switched sights.

Haze blackened the room. I tuned it out, brought vision into focus.

The tall figure was smiling at me. He held a gun in his hand.

The crowd screamed.

I saw his finger squeeze down on the trigger.

A searing pain struck my chest; I was being torn apart. I

crashed against the wall. As I fell, I saw Pabst step out of the crowd, reach for his gun . . .

The girl's words came to me as though from a long distance.

"You have exhausted your time."

I licked dry lips with an even drier tongue. I could feel the sweat standing out on my forehead, soaking my shirt. I could hardly breathe.

"You're right," I whispered in a hoarse voice. "It was me."

"Die, assassin!" the girl hissed.

"But it's not me anymore."

"It is you! You!"

I shook my head weakly. "Didn't Van-See tell you? Amtroy, the guard captain—or whoever he was—is dead forever, his memory lost—wiped clean. Only his body is still kicking around—for whatever that's worth."

"You take me for a fool? If you are innocent, why did you so desperately seek to defend the guard captain, this 'stranger' of whom you claim to have no recollection?"

I sighed. "Because I was hoping he might still turn out to be me. Because I didn't want to become the man whose memories I *do* have."

"And who is that, pig?"

"Your father."

The girl's lips curled back in a snarl. "You are the lowest of the low!"

"I'm sorry. I didn't plan it that way. Van-See recorded your father's memory before he died, pinned the XI tape to my sleeve as I lay unconscious. My own mind was erased, but the Chairman's memories filtered through. It's a bum deal for both of us; you've lost your old man, I've lost me."

"You are *not* my father!"

"I wish to God I wasn't. Listen: when you were nine, you broke your wrist; I sat up with you all night. At age ten, I bought you a silk party gown. It was bright red and reached to the floor. I made a speech a year later to the Galactic Council and you gave me a couple of ideas for it. No one knew except us. You told me about a dream you had when you were fifteen. It had to do with your becoming an Empress. When you were sixteen you wanted to go to the jungle world of Urga. I wouldn't let you—too dangerous. You threatened to run away. At eighteen you had your first fling—with one of the Council pageboys. I canned him. When you hit twenty—"

"Enough! It is not possible. You sound *nothing* like my father."

"There's more than one voice in me, Adinah. There were dreams I had: about this house, this city, about being killed —and the voice in the dreams wasn't mine. Your father used lots of XI tapes. There was more than one voice floating around in his head. Maybe I just haven't learned to control them yet."

"But Van-See said nothing."

"He wouldn't. Knowing who I was could've made you slip up, accidentally tip off the opposition. It'd've been curtains for both of us then."

"Oh, yes indeed," a voice said from the darkened passage-way in the wall. "Oh dear yes, that is *exactly* how it was."

Van-See and Lix-el stepped into the room.

"My dear friends," Van-See said, rubbing his hands together, "it is so good to see you both safe and sound. Forgive me, I could not help but overhear part of your conversation."

"He waited," Lix-el said dryly, "by the door, to make certain."

"My curiosity is, alas, insatiable," Van-See said.

"It is true?" the girl asked. "That he is my father?"

"Yes, my child." Van-See shrugged. "I had no choice." To me he said, "Forgive my deception, dear friend. It seemed senseless to burden you with this deed; it was not done by you, only your body. You would have known of it in any case once you came to yourself."

"Yeah, came to myself. What brings you here—we holding a convention?"

"When you and the girl didn't return," Lix-el said, "it seemed wise to investigate."

"The rescue squad, huh? Thanks. You won't get me to complain."

Van-See jerked a thumb toward the phony Chairman. "What in the world has happened?"

"She shot him," I said.

The girl had lowered her laser. It was now pointed at the floor, a nice, safe target. She looked at us wearily.

"My child," Van-See said, "you must be brave. After all, your dear father still lives."

This Van-See was getting on my nerves.

Lix-el turned to me. "The figurehead's demise changes things. We must move now, sir, bring the Legion into play."

"Yeah, you're right. We ought to stuff him in a closet, get the hell out of here. Think your Legion can handle this job?"

"I don't know, sir; Fas-Ten is overly cautious. I have yet to take full inventory of our resources. But one thing is certain —we are not likely to find a better time. Confusion will reign here for the present. And the return of your memory can aid us greatly in achieving our goals."

"It can. But don't count on it."

"I beg your pardon, sir?"

"My mind, Lix-el. It's still a mess."

"But my dear boy," Van-See said, "you did just wonderfully a moment ago."

"You mean that stuff about Adinah. Yeah, I rattled off a mouthful, didn't I?"

The girl spoke, her voice listless. "Everything you said was quite correct."

"Sure. Some stunt. Only a second before I said it, I didn't know any of it."

"Even so—" Van-See began.

"Listen. A lot of memories bob right to the surface. But others don't. I've got to wade through a lot of junk sometimes, and I never know what I'll come up with."

Lix-el said, "You will not help us?"

"That's not what I'm saying. Sure I will. But I'm not reliable. I don't have the Chairman's memories down pat. If you bet everything on my having the answers, we'll have a flop on our hands."

"Understood," Lix-el said.

"He is not my father," the girl burst out. "He neither speaks nor thinks like my father. There is some *terrible* error here."

"Now, now, my *dear* child," Van-See said. "This is surely not—"

"Yeah, we've got to hustle. Let's roll Fatso into the passageway and beat it."

"A pleasure," Lix-el said, getting busy. I helped him carry the body.

"Who pulled his strings?" I said. "Who ran the Chairman?"

"Pabst," Van-See said.

"Where is he?"

"Dear me, I have no idea."

"We'd better find him fast," I said, "and take him out of play. *Before he finds us.*"

Van-See said, "I once had an office in this very building."

"You don't say?" I said.

Van-See rubbed his hands together, grinned at me. "No doubt it is now occupied by my successor."

"No doubt, sir," Lix-el said.

"We should visit it," Van-See said.

"Feeling homesick?" I said. "Or just want to give us the tour?"

"Neither, my dear friend. Unless things have greatly changed during my absence, we shall find a duty roster there. It will not only give us Pabst's whereabouts, but also tell us who else is in charge."

"Invaluable, sir," Lix-el said. "We must make the effort."

"My child," Van-See told the girl, "what we do now may prove dangerous. You have been through enough. Use the passageway. Return to Ken-Rue's. You have earned a rest, I should think."

"He is quite right," Lix-el said.

"No," the girl said.

"My dear—" Van-See began.

"My place is here," the girl said. "I shall avenge my father."

"Not that again," I complained.

"I wish to confront Pabst—myself!" she said.

Van-See rubbed his hands together. "Headstrong, like her father."

"You sure?" I asked her.

"Yes."

"Okay. That's settled."

Van-See sighed. "Follow me," he said, heading out into the corridor. "Be careful."

We followed. We were careful as all get-out.

The sirens caught us midway to our destination. At first they came from outside, somewhere off in the city. Then all hell broke loose in the mansion itself.

"What *is* it?" the girl yelled.

"Don't ask me," I yelled back. "I'm just tagging along after Van-See here." I turned to the ex-adviser. "We trip a spotter-eye or something? This can't be for us."

"It's not. Those are raid sirens. The Capital is under assault."

Over the siren's din, we heard shouting voices, running feet headed our way. I slid my gun loose.

A squad of guards rounded a corner, came tearing up the hallway. They didn't give us a second glance.

"The viewer hall," Van-See yelled.

We followed the guard's example, broke into a trot. Van-See led the way.

A babble of voices greeted us as we approached the hall. We were going to have lots of company. We barged right through the swinging double doors. No one paid the least attention to us. This crowd had other things on their minds.

Viewscreens lined the walls.

Most, I saw, showed peaceful sights out in the city.

One didn't.

The crowd was busy milling around this viewer.

I looked up at the large screen too. And got an eyeful.

Men and creatures were pouring out of a house. They wore black uniforms. They carried weapons. They moved like soldiers. But their faces were all pasty white. Their eyes seemed glazed. And they looked neither to left nor right.

A squad of Galactic guards had gone up against them. The black-clad troops didn't seem to mind.

They ignored lasers. Bullets didn't faze them. Unless blasted to smithereens, they just kept coming, arms shot off, legs in pieces, heads all but dangling from their necks.

I recognized this crew, all right, there was no way to mistake them.

Blanks.

But not mere Blanks.

Blanks. And something else.

Their departure point was familiar too. I had been there less than eight hours ago. The troops were spilling out of the corner house, the one with the transmitter stashed in it.

I whispered to Lix-el, "Let's get out of here."

The four of us got.

The hidden passage which ran the mansion's length wasn't silent anymore. The siren's blare found its way even here. We hurried along under the row of dim glowers.

Van-See said, "There is nothing to fear."

"Nothing, huh?"

"The Capital is quite impregnable."

"Not against these babies," I said.

The girl said, "They are Blanks, are they not?"

"That's what they are," I said.

"Preposterous," Van-See said.

Lix-el said, "Blanks, sir, cannot fight. They have difficulties in performing even the simplest physical tasks."

"Tell me something I don't know," I said.

"Then, why do you insist on calling them Blanks?"

"Because that's what they are."

"He was one of them," the girl said.

"Yeah. That makes me the expert around here. And those babies are Blanks."

"Then how do you explain their combat abilities?" Lix-el asked.

"I don't."

"Or their capacity, my dear boy, to withstand punishment?" Van-See said.

"Can't explain that either. All I know is that they're Blanks. And we'd better plug that hole they're coming through, or this whole Capital will be buried under 'em."

"Hole?" Van-See said.

"Transmitter," I said.

"My dear boy," Van-See said breathlessly. "You *know* the location of the fabled transmitter?"

"Yeah."

"What, sir, is a transmitter?" Lix-el said.

Van-See said, "It was only rumored to exist. It provides instantaneous transmission. I had no idea—"

"I knew," the girl said.

"You would," I said. "You're the exception. The Chairman liked his little secrets, played his cards close to his vest. That's what gave him the upper hand."

The girl said, "You can stop the invaders—with the transmitter?"

"It's what they're using to get here," I said. "Possibly I can gum up the works somehow. I don't know. I've got to look over the system, see if anything clicks into place."

"Then, my dear boy, you are not certain," Van-See said.

"Yeah, that's what I am, not certain. Better keep your fingers crossed."

Up ahead I saw the light coming from the small, dusty transmitter room. We were lucky in one way, at least. The invaders didn't know about this platform, or they'd have been swarming all over the place. Maybe there were other things they didn't know.

I could still hear the sirens raising a racket.

I put on the steam, sprinted the last steps, swung into the room.

He was standing by the platform, a slender man of medium height, with his hands stuck in his coat pockets.

"Hiya, Nick," he said.

— CHAPTER —
Thirty-Six

Block nodded at the four figures who stood before him.

"Adinah," he said. "Van-See. And you would be Lix-el. Just like old home week, isn't it?"

"And you, sir?"

Block shrugged. *The Chairman.*

"Dear, oh dear, but that is *quite* impossible," Van-See blurted out. "*He* is the Chairman."

"Yeah," Nick Siscoe said. "That's me, the Chairman. But if you want the prize, it's all yours, brother."

"Really?" Block said. "How'd you become Chairman, Nick?"

Nick Siscoe hesitated, looked closely at Block, grinned, said, "Sure, why not? Van-See here. They were going to erase me. But Van-See switched tapes on 'em. They fed me the Chairman's memory instead."

"How much," Block asked, "do you remember?"

"Bits and pieces. And you, pal, how'd *you* become Chairman?"

Block smiled. "I haven't got all of it. But I can give you a pretty good guess. Pabst saw Van-See drag the Chairman off to the transfer room, followed him. Van-See must've made more than one copy of the Chairman's memory. Probably figured on using it himself. Pabst stole it.

"The Chairman and Pabst had a little something going for them on Earth. Earth was off limits, in a restricted part of the universe. The Galactic Council wouldn't've stood for an outright invasion. Even the Chairman wasn't that all-powerful. But with the help of the transmitter, the Chairman and Pabst had set up shop on Earth. That section of the universe was due for reclassification soon; it would be up for grabs. The Chairman was getting a head start. Pabst—through an outfit called McCoy—ran a network of agents, one that covered the globe. They were worming their way into the right places. When the time came, Earth would be a plum ripe for picking.

"The coup wasn't Pabst's idea; he was slated to be one of its victims. But the guys behind the push didn't know about the transmitter, about Earth. Pabst grabbed the Chairman's XI tape and took off for Earth.

"This Pabst was a pretty slick article. But he should've paid more attention to his henchmen. One of his stooges, an old pal of yours, Nick—Marty Nash—jumped Pabst, made off with the Chairman's XI tape before Pabst could use it himself. Nash didn't know what he had, but he figured it must be worth plenty. He carried it to a hideout of his, took a gander. You know what that does, Nick; it screws up your mind. Pabst found Nash wandering around the city. He put him through the wringer, but it didn't help much. Nash couldn't remember. He got nailed trying to escape.

"I'm a reporter, Nick; I started snooping around the Nash case, stumbled across the Chairman's tape. That's how I came by his memories."

"Some story," Siscoe said. "So who's this Nick you've been calling me?"

"Nick Siscoe. I'll fill you in. But what's all the racket out there? You folks having a fire drill? Or is that for real?"

"That, sir," Lix-el said, "is an invasion."

"Oh dear, yes," Van-See said, rubbing his hands together. "While we stand here and chat, our Capital is being assaulted!"

"By whom?" Block asked.

"Blanks," Nick Siscoe said. "Blanks fixed up to act like soldiers. They're pouring out of the transmitter. They take what you throw at 'em, and come back for more. They're damn tough to kill."

Block stood very still for a moment, shook his head. "Tough isn't the word. Impossible is more like it."

"They are the dead," the girl said.

A half-smile appeared on Ross Block's face. "See? She guessed. The Chairman was very fond of his daughter, liked to confide in her. Didn't he, Adinah?"

"What in the world, sir, are you talking about?" Lix-el demanded.

"The Planet of the Dead. A little surprise the Chairman was saving up. Frozen corpses. And X2 warrior tapes to run them. Its location is supposed to be top secret."

"So it was, my friend," a voice said in Block's mind. *"But I plucked it out of the gladiator's brain."*

Block said, "Anyone here a gladiator?"

"Me again," Siscoe said.

"Know any telepaths, Nick?"

"Yeah, one. Ganz. He helped us crash out of stir."

Block said, "I'm afraid you've gone and spilled the beans, Nick. The Chairman always figured Ganz for a menace. That's why he sent him up."

"Ganz is here?" Siscoe said.

"Here," Block said. "Along with his dead."

"I have yearned for this moment, my friend; it is a pity you will not live long enough to see me proclaimed Emperor."

Block said, "He says he's going to be Emperor. And I'm headed for a slab."

"Not merely you," Ganz said, *"the rest as well."*

"Why?" Block said.

"Collectively, you would be a threat to me. Your knowledge is too vast. Surely you see that?"

"Says we know too much. Wants to kill us all."

"He must be stopped!" Van-See shrieked.

"That's not a bad idea," Block said.

"Fools," Ganz said.

"Nick, you come with me."

"You're leaving us?" Van-See shouted.

"You're safe here," Block said. "The Galactic troops will defend this place to the last man. We'll be back before you know it."

"But you can't—" Van-See screamed.

"Got to. Nick?"

Siscoe and Block stepped on the platform. Block turned a knob, then another.

They vanished.

They were in total darkness.

Block fished around in his pocket for matches, struck a light.

They were on a transmitter platform. The room was very small, windowless, stuffy and covered by dust.

"Cozy," Siscoe said.

He found the light switch. Dim glowers shone feebly. "Where the hell are we?" he asked.

"Still on the Control World," Block said, "but halfway around the globe."

"Right. Now what're we doing here?"

"Trying to keep one jump ahead of Ganz. I've got to plot a course to the Planet of the Dead. No direct transmission from here. The Chairman was being cagey. Even Pabst didn't know for sure the planet existed, let alone how to reach it."

Siscoe said, "But *you* know."

"Uh-huh. We hop from platform to platform. We go halfway across the universe till we hit the right transmitter. From there it's a snap."

Block was standing on the platform, hands thrust in pockets, one shoulder leaning against the wall.

Siscoe said, "And that's what you're up to—plotting this course?"

"Yep."

"Oh brother. In your head? While you're talking?"

"Sure. The Chairman was a whiz. He fed himself so many learning tapes, he could've beat a stadium full of quiz kids. Ask me anything."

"How come you remember and I don't?"

Block grinned. "I was in the same boat as you, Nick. My first squint at an XI tape knocked me on my ear. It was just a glimpse, that saved me. I wasn't as lucky the second time I looked. It scrambled my brain like an eggbeater. Bits of my life, the Chairman's, and lots of tapes he'd been fed whirled around my brain. I knew someone was hunting me, and— after I picked myself off the floor that second time—left my apartment, found an Upper East Side flat to hide out in till I came to myself. Every week I'd take a peek at the tape, go under again. But I was getting used to it, see? By then I figured I wasn't nuts. And I was learning more each time. I thought I had it licked, and that was my big mistake. I flipped both lids off. Oh, yes, there were two tapes in that box. I took a bath in the white light. And when I woke up I was almost a Blank. I landed on the Bowery, Nick, a bum. But the Chairman's memory was in my mind, and it started coming back. You'll get it back, too, Nick. You were fed the Chairman in one gulp. That's too much. It kept you woozy. But I was exposed gradually. And that's what made the difference."

"Yeah," Siscoe said, "I get it. We're both the Chairman. Great. Now who's this Nick Siscoe?"

"You were a hood, Nick."

"Thought I was a gladiator."

"Boxer, for a while. Martin Nash was your pal. You were both in the rackets together. And you both ended up at McCoy. Pabst took a liking to your wife, Sal. The Chairman needed a new bodyguard. Amtroy, his old one, had gotten himself bumped off. Pabst—he called himself Charles Hastings on Earth—put you on a platform, transmitted you here. He fixed Amtroy's body so no one would recognize it, and then used the stiff to stage an accident that would account for your 'death.' You became the captain of the guards."

"And I didn't beef?"

"It was aces with you, Nick, a whooping promotion. Think of the wonders you got to see."

"Yeah, but—"

"Foolish little men, with your foolish little schemes. Did you really think you could escape me? You are helpless against me. I could have destroyed the gladiator at will back on the penal world; he trusted me. But I had to be certain that the army of the dead still functioned. If not, my best option lay with the gladiator himself, helping him regain power. As his ally it would have been only a matter of time before I took total control. Now that is unnecessary. The dead are my legions."

"Come on, Nick," Block said. "It's Ganz. His mind's caught up with us. Let's scram."

"Futile. You are as children against my powers. You have no chance . . ."

"Screw you," Block said.

Siscoe stepped on the platform.

They vanished.

Reappeared in an empty, white-walled hall.

"Fools," Ganz echoed.

Vanished.

Popped up in an underground cavern.

"Fools," Ganz bawled.

Vanished.

And materialized in a small stone cottage near a forest.

"Shook him," Siscoe said.

Block said, "Let's finish the trip."

Bar stood before the final transmitter and grinned.

"Sorry," he said.

He held a blaster in one large hand.

Pale light shone through the cracked windows of the ancient Temple of Kardue. Weeds sprouted through cracks in the floor. The cries of wild birds could be heard outdoors.

"Last stop," Bar rumbled.

"Ganz?" Block said.

"He thought you might come this way," Bar said.

Siscoe threw himself at the giant, grabbed his gun arm.

Bar smiled.

He shook his arm and Siscoe fell off.

Siscoe got to his feet, kicked Bar in the guts, smashed a right into his face.

Bar swung a huge arm.

Siscoe spun across the room.

Block kicked out.

The tip of his shoe sliced into Bar's throat. Block drove a finger into Bar's right eye, ripped downward.

The giant screamed.

"Shoot him, for God's sake," Block shrieked.

By then, Nick Siscoe had his laser out. He shot him.

"Jesus," Block said.

Siscoe was breathing hard. "Let's go pull the plug," he said.

— CHAPTER —
Thirty-Seven

"The shooting's stopped," Lix-el said.

"Yeah," I said. "Ganz had a pair of goons feeding X2 tapes to the stiffs. We blasted 'em. And that was that."

"All the Galactic boys have to do now is mop up," Block said. "They'll get Ganz too."

"Dear me, yes," Van-See said. "How can I ever express my gratitude?"

"That's going to be tough," Block said.

"I beg your pardon?"

"Like I told Nick," Block said, "there were two tapes in Pabst's box. I was exposed to both. One was the Chairman's. Guess who belonged to the other?"

Van-See shrugged, rubbed his hands together. "But how can I?"

"Easy," Block said. "You're the guy who recorded it. You got Nick to assassinate the Chairman, promised to set him up for life. And Nick bought it. He got his memories down on the XI tape first, just in case there was a foulup. You put the Chairman's tape next to his in a little metal box. Pabst ran off with both."

"Don't tell me," I said.

"Yes, Nick," Block said. "I'm you."